Treasures
Visible & Invisible

By Catholic Teen Books Authors:

Theresa Linden
Susan Peek
Antony B. Kolenc
Amanda Lauer
Carolyn Astfalk
Leslea Wahl
T. M. Gaouette
Corinna Turner

Praise for *Treasures*

In a world where today's young adults are constantly surrounded by media that is trying desperately to tear them down, it is a blessing to have books like this that reaffirm our Catholic faith. Not only does each author give us a great story to read, they also challenge us to think about things like: the hardships of people in our ancient church, putting Grandma first on our social calendars, praying to God when in the midst of fear and suffering, staying strong in our faith while looking death in the face, listening to unlikely friends who lead us on the path to Christ, and ultimately realizing there is sacredness in the relics of our church. You only find stories that build our faith like this in very special books. The "building-up" of today's youth is at the very heart and soul of what the authors are trying to do here, and they have done an amazing job.

Beth Ruggiero
Lit by the Tree, Literature reviews from the Catholic side.
Litbythetree.com

I invite teens, and readers of all ages, to stand on the craggy wind-swept cliff of your imagination, and experience the collection of stories called, Treasures: Visible & Invisible, *created by the talented team of authors from Catholic Teen Books. With a shamrock as our touchstone, this book takes us on a journey through an expanse of time from ancient to modern. Be inspired by the holy greatness of heroism rooted in the spiritual treasures of the Emerald Isle.*

Cathy Gilmore,
Creator and advocator of stories that inspire heroic virtue.
VirtueHeroes.com

We thoroughly enjoyed this cleverly written book about the intercession of Saint Patrick throughout the ages. The combination of dynamic characters and intriguing stories kept us hooked from start to finish. A valuable addition to your Saint Patrick's Day bookshelf!

**Jennifer & Kate Waldyke,
Co-hosts of Catholic Mom and Daughter**

This is the third collection from the authors of Catholic Teen Books. It was an inspiring read. Some stories are of miracles and others about change. Two contributors from the previous collection did not contribute and two new ones have joined the fray. In this collection are 8 stories from the 14 authors who currently compose the collective. My first thought was wow! What an amazing collection of stories around Saint Patrick! I am aware that not everyone likes short stories, but I love them, and this collection is amazing! Short stories are a different art form than novels, and not all novelists have mastered the craft. For a short story to be good, the writing needs to be tighter, cleaner, and crisper. And each of the 8 in this collection is extremely well written…

**(Full review on BookReviewsAndMore.ca)
Steven R. McEvoy, BookReviewsAndMore.ca**

What a gift to Catholic teens and their families! Each piece in this collection of stories revolving around St Patrick is a beautiful portrayal of the faith. These are wholesome, engaging, and inspiring tales from a variety of genres that will both entertain and spiritually nourish every reader who picks up this book.

Katie Fitzgerald, ReadAtHomeMom.com

~~~✝~~~
~~~

DEDICATION

For Saint Patrick, who in his autobiography, *Saint Patrick's Confessio*, wrote, "I know for certain, that before I was humbled I was like a stone lying in deep mire, and He that is mighty came and in His mercy raised me up and, indeed, lifted me high up and placed me on top of the wall."

CONTENTS

"The kingdom of heaven is like treasure
hidden in a field, which a man found and covered up;
then in his joy he goes and sells all that he has and
buys that field."
(Matthew 13:44 RSV-CE)

4th Century, Ireland

TREASURE IN THE BOGS

by Theresa Linden

Magonus Saccatus stroked the soft fur of his favorite lamb and eased the warm little creature off his lap. Giving up on waiting for his friends Cillian and Tag, he got up from the boulder, secured his cape against the wind with a leather tie at his shoulder, and headed down the grassy, rocky hillside to find them. They'd planned to meet here around noon before heading off together for the festival marking the end of the harvest season, the Eve of Samhain. Celebrations all day and well into the night, they'd said, with music on the harp and horn, storytelling—of pagan gods, of course—but also sports competitions, food, and goods for sale. He had no money to buy anything, but he'd enjoy the experience.

An uncomfortable inner voice raised a question. What would his parents think if they knew he was celebrating this pagan festival? His father—not just a Roman officer but a deacon in the Church, and his mother related to the saintly bishop of Tours. Not to mention he had other ordained relatives. His parents had likely been aware of his lack of faith, but they didn't pester him about it. They'd probably hoped that one day . . .

Magonus stomped down the hill at a quicker pace. It didn't matter. He'd probably never see them again. Would he ever escape from this place? How could he?

Annoyed at the direction his life had taken, Magonus rubbed the long scar on his neck, where an iron collar had once cut into his skin. He remembered the first day of his captivity. Three months ago; he had not yet turned fifteen. He and his family had just arrived at their summer home on the western coast of Roman Briton, near the village of Bannavern Taburniae.

Anxious to meet up with a close friend, Magonus jogged toward the shore, just glimpsing it through the trees. He hadn't seen his friend in several months, since just after he'd shared his deepest secret with him. Maybe he shouldn't have told anyone at all, but his low mood at the time had him spilling things he would've otherwise kept to himself. It hadn't been that big of a deal. Had it? Even though it still troubled his thoughts now and then. It had only concerned some things he'd done one day—rather, in one little hour.

As Magonus slowed his pace to catch his breath, he marveled at the pink sky, but in the next moment he realized he should've taken it as an omen. A shriek pierced the calm, and a flutter of seagulls took to the air. More panic-stricken screams followed.

His gaze snapped to the shore, still barely visible between foliage.

His mother's last words to him had been, "Keep an eye on the coast."

Roman legions had once protected them from invaders, but they'd been departing squad by squad, called away to defend other regions of the Roman Empire, leaving them vulnerable to raids by warriors dispatched by Ireland's King Niall of the Nine Hostages. Magonus, and every other boy, had heard of him. He was the High King who lived in the center of Ireland and who fearlessly battled the English, French, Scots, and Romans.

Could it be? Regardless of his parents' repeated warnings, Magonus had never expected the threat to come close to home.

Little flecks swirled in his peripheral vision, and a campfire smell tickled his nose. He spun to look back the way he'd come. Trees blocked his view of the family estate and other nearby homes, clouds of dark smoke rising above them, one cloud here, one there.

Magonus' heart thumped out of control and sweat broke out on his skin. Something was wrong. Danger like he'd never known before. He'd better get back to the estate.

Before he could even turn, solid arms snaked around him from behind, gripped him hard, and hoisted him off his feet.

A few minutes later, he sat chained to other captives on wet wicker slats running the length of a long boat, amidst dozens of other currachs in the sea off the western coast of Roman Briton, heading for Ireland, the land of druids and pagans.

Keeping an eye out for Cillian and Tag, Magonus passed a decorative stone that stood as tall and wide as he did. Swirling patterns adorned the stone. They must've meant something—maybe warded off evil spirits or some such nonsense—but Magonus had yet to figure it out. He thumped across a little bridge that stretched over a ditch and then past a wooden fence, both of which surrounded the homestead, protecting it from raiders. Two round houses with pointy thatched roofs stood in the center of the ringfort, the larger one made of stones, the smaller of skins stretched over wicker posts. Servants milled about the fort, one tending the hens and geese, another hanging clothes on a line, a third grinding grain by the smaller house. The others had likely gone to the festival already.

Magonus glimpsed his friend Rhona, a servant girl his age, delivering rations. She met his gaze with red-rimmed eyes and turned away. Pity stirred in Magonus' heart, though he had no idea what bothered her. None of them had it easy as the servants of Milchu, a chieftain and a druid. Magonus had met Rhona his first day here. She'd brought him a meager food supply—goose eggs, apples, and flatbread—that he'd had to make stretch out for a week. His stomach growled now at the thought of food. He never got enough to eat or drink and envied the sheep, who could satisfy themselves on the plentiful grass and clover of the land.

Two cows grazed at the opposite end of the fort. Farmers had brought them to the druid, hoping for cures. Many cows had been coming down with something lately, some of them dying. Magonus doubted that Milchu would be able to help them, but the people had trust in the druid. Strange what people put their faith in.

Reaching the servants' skin-covered house, Magonus

flung open the door. Pale sunlight streamed in from an opening in the cone-shaped roof, falling on the straw-littered dirt floor, the cooking stones in the center, and the empty pallets along the walls.

"Tag?" Magonus whispered. While the house looked empty, Cillian had always found places to hide Tag, the red-headed nine-year-old cripple. Magonus approached a stack of wooden bowls, earthen pots, and jugs and whispered the boy's name again. He'd grown fond of the boy, just as Cillian had, and would never want any bad to come to him. But not everyone felt the same way. So Cillian kept the boy hidden and shared his meager rations with him, stealing more for the thin little boy when he could.

"He's gone."

Magonus jumped at the sound of the feminine voice coming from the half-open door behind him. "Greetings, Rhona."

Pushing a lock of thick auburn hair off her freckled face, she gazed at him through sad gray eyes that matched the color of her long wool cloak. "They found him," she whispered, her voice cracking. "He'd gone out early this morning to . . . "

"Found whom?" A dizzying sensation overcame him as his mind gave him the answer. "They found him this morning?"

"Kept him tied up until Milchu decided what to do with him. Messengers came and went. Then a party of druids"—her voice broke—"took him away. Then . . . then

Cillian went to rescue him. He thinks they took him to the bogs."

"The bogs? Why?"

"The cows . . . " She pressed her thin lips together as if unable to speak without crying but then tipped her round chin upward, perhaps trying to steel herself. Rhona, like many of the Irish slaves, had both a calmness and an inner strength that kept them going day after day. "They hope to save the cows."

Magonus understood well enough. The druids offered sacrifices and votive offerings at the bogs to appease the gods or to secure blessings and favors. Some offerings consisted of shields and helmets, coins, jewelry or other valuables, and even animals. Other offerings made no sense. Little carved statues, bog idols. But other offerings . . . those made Magonus' head spin. How could they sacrifice a human being to something that didn't really exist? There were no gods. There was no God.

"Criminals and cripples," Rhona managed to say, offering more of an explanation as to why they would sacrifice Tag.

Cillian had told him about that. Shortly after receiving his shepherd's staff and being shown the hill where he was expected to spend the rest of his days tending sheep, Magonus had decided to escape.

"I'm sorry, to disappoint you," he said to the flock of sheep standing close together like a big ball of fleece, *"but I've got to flee. I have no intention of being a shepherd in Ireland my whole*

life."

Not knowing his way around, he headed in the direction in which he'd seen Milchu, the druid, depart, hoping to arrive at some well-traveled road. Instead, Magonus found Milchu in a grove with other druids, all of them with long white beards and pale hooded capes. They chanted and danced around a roaring bonfire and tall, sharp stones set upright in a circle.

"This is not a good night to be out."

Magonus jumped at the sound of the voice whispering over his shoulder.

Laughing without making a sound, Cillian pulled Magonus to the ground, probably to avoid the druids' notice. "This is the Summer Solstice, the holy day of Litha. Faeries and ghosts are out and about tonight. And some claim to see them."

"See them? Impossible. There's no such thing—"

Cillian—a year or two older than Magonus but with a build twice as sturdy—put a dirt-stained finger to his thin lips, silencing Magonus. "You don't believe because you don't see them yourself, huh?" The older boy peered through the brush in the direction of the druids. Their chants and a campfire odor wafted on the warm night air. "The hours of light are as long as they will ever be, and the power of the sun weakens when the days grow shorter. So the druids' bonfire adds to the sun's energy."

Magonus shook his head. He grew up on other tales. Water becoming wine. Wine becoming blood. Healings and miracles and a man rising from the dead. Everyone had to believe in something, he guessed. It made life bearable. Magonus got his feet back under him and stood.

Cillian rose with him. "Look, I know you want to run off, but please don't." His expression had turned harder than the stones around which the druids chanted. "If you run, you will become a criminal. And even if they don't catch you—which they will—you have nothing to pay your ship fare."

"I don't care if I become a criminal." Turning away from Cillian, whom he had yet to think of as a friend, he peered at the druids through the brush.

"Criminals and cripples," Cillian said. "That's who the druids prefer to offer when the gods require human sacrifice."

On their walk back to the flock, Cillian had explained about the bogs, where most sacrifices and votive offerings took place. Magonus had seen them for himself in the days following, at a distance, anyway, while tending sheep on Mis's Mountain. After a steep and rocky climb, the low mountain gave him a view of forests and fields, bogs and even the coast and sea beyond the bogs.

Rhona stood gazing at Magonus, as if wondering what he might do to help their friends.

"How long ago did Cillian set off after him?" Magonus finally said. "Did he follow immediately?"

"I don't know." Still standing in the doorway, Rhona glanced over her shoulder at the partially cloudy sky. "He's been gone for over an hour, I'd say."

Despair forced an involuntary exhale from Magonus. Blaming himself for not looking for his friends sooner, he clenched a fist.

Rhona stepped through the doorway toward him, a

glimmer of hope in her gray eyes. "This night stands on the boundary between the old year and the new one."

Put off by her pagan beliefs and not wanting to hear more, he turned away. "Yes, Cillian told me all about it." As fall came to an end, the old year passed away and the new began. The pagans believed that the barriers between the worlds of the living and the dead temporarily disappeared. The dead arose and would walk the earth. Tonight. One of their goddesses, Morrigan, would take the shape of a raven and guide the dying back to the otherworld. "I don't want Tag among the dying tonight."

What could he possibly do about it at this moment? Frustration overcoming him, he shoved a stack of clay pots and dishes with his foot. They clattered to the hard-packed earthen floor with a sound that rattled through him.

"Listen, I'm trying to tell you . . . They won't sacrifice him until the sun meets the land, the boundary between sky and earth."

Still facing away from her, Magonus drew a breath and held it. Dare he hope? Tag could still be alive. Gaining resolve, he turned to the door and strode past her. "I'm going after them."

With only his shepherd's staff, Magonus made his way down a rocky path littered with fresh footprints and cart tracks, through a forest of willow and birch trees. A strong wind blew, rattling the leaves, creaking through branches, and tousling his hood and cape. He'd never come this way before—in fact, he rarely strayed from the flock at all—but from the top of Mis's Mountain, he'd seen the lay of the surrounding area and the trails that led to the bogs. It shouldn't take him long to reach them. The bogs covered a good bit of land but maybe as he drew near, he'd spot signs of the druid party. Perhaps he'd find them. And then what would he do?

Magonus glanced at his shepherd's staff as he took his next step. Could he use it as a weapon? He couldn't lose his only friends. When he'd first arrived in Ireland, he'd known nothing of these people's language. Milchu had nearly turned blue in the face trying to boss Magonus around, until he realized that Cillian could translate. Cillian came from Roman Briton, just as Magonus had, only two years earlier. The two soon became friends—and Tag and Rhona too. And while Magonus didn't get to see them often, it had been enough to keep him from feeling utterly alone. The shepherd that Magonus replaced had died over the winter, from the cold and from hunger, Cillian had said. But Magonus thought loneliness might've contributed to his demise as well.

As he journeyed onward, the trail went one way and then another, mostly over flat land. The sun, peeking through clouds, hovered to his left and then before him, then back to his left as the path turned again.

The woods thinned out, a splotchy green landscape becoming visible between tree trunks. Magonus' feet sunk into the muddied path. The footprints and cart tracks he'd noticed before no longer showed themselves in the watery muck. Almost an hour after setting out, the sun had dropped significantly lower in the cloudy sky. He'd been watching it the whole way, willing it to slow down. He needed to find Tag before sunset.

How had Milchu discovered him? After trying unsuccessfully to cure the cows, he'd probably seen the crippled boy as the answer to his prayers. If he could offer up the child, he could appease the gods and save the cows. How stupid of the druids to think that sacrificing a person could accomplish anything.

His mind went back to the catechism his father had tried teaching him over the years. The Son of God came to earth to be the sacrifice for sin. Magonus dismissed the thought. Suffering and misfortune, common to everyone, made people desperate to make sense of it. So they created religious beliefs that gave value to anguish and sacrifices.

Magonus' entire existence had become one great misfortune. Ripped from his family. A slave to a pagan chieftain. Weak from hunger almost every day. Shivering in the cold every night. Completely alone, not counting the sheep. He had no place even to lay his head at night, like the other servants who slept in the wicker and skin houses.

What purpose could all that suffering serve? If there were a God, why would He allow it? If there were a God, He must've been a distant one who didn't care about people. If that were the case, Magonus would rather believe He didn't exist at all.

Glimpsing something strange up ahead, Magonus slowed his stride. A waist-high statue with a rough imitation of a face carved into it—two deep eyes, a long nose, and a line for a grim mouth—stood off to the side as if guarding a sacred area. Was this one of their gods? He saw no sign of druids, or anyone else, for that matter.

Cillian, Tag, and Rhona had told him about numerous gods and goddesses. One offered protection against enemies, one was a god of thunder, and one even had three faces. Magonus had told them that he didn't understand why they worshipped all those man-made gods. Rhona had asked what he believed in. The faith that he'd been taught as a child came to mind, but the answer that spouted from his lips was, "I don't believe in anything."

Beyond the statue, the path faded into a large wetland of green moss and grass. Curvy waterways and pools created big and little islands of peat and moss and reflected the pinks, blues, and yellows in the sky. A breeze ruffled the longer tufts of grass, giving motion to the otherwise still scene. So beautiful and haunting at the same time. A simple glance could not reveal what lay hidden in the bogs.

His gaze lifted to the horizon, and he sucked in his breath. Magonus' heart pounded so hard and fast that he felt it in his throat. The yellow orb of sun had dropped even more, preparing now to kiss the horizon. He was running out of time! Tag was running out of time! Where could the druids possibly be?

Magonus sprinted for the bog. Keeping to the grassy areas and solid land and careful to avoid the calm waters reflecting the sunset, he weaved his way through the maze of the bog. He glanced up between steps, his gaze searching the distance until he spotted something. A cluster of flames glowed in the distance. Torches. It had to be Milchu and the other druids. Maybe their ceremony would consist of other things—chanting and dancing and who knew what—before they offered . . . the sacrifice.

Please help me. I must get there in time. As soon as the prayer stirred in his heart, he dismissed it. He'd only uttered it in desperation. He didn't really believe anyone would hear it.

Magonus leaped over a wider pool to a thin strip of moss-covered land. His foot slipped. And his heart shot to his throat. But as his toe dipped in the water, he thrust himself forward and landed awkwardly on the next patch of earth. With no time to even catch his balance, he sprang forward again to another bit of spongy land.

The wind whistled through the wetland, sometimes rising above the sound of his own breathing and the thumping of his feet, but presently a musical note carried over the bogs. Someone in the distance blew a horn, perhaps a bronze *dord* like the one that Milchu often carried with him. The low timbre cut through Magonus' heart, overcoming him with grief, with failure.

He glanced up and scanned the sky, looking for what? The goddess of death in the form of a raven, coming to lead Tag to the Otherworld? No, he did not believe in that.

What if he didn't get there in time? He couldn't go back to Milchu. Not after this. Not after knowing that Milchu had murdered little Tag. No, he wouldn't go back. How many votive offerings lay hidden in the bogs? Coins, gold, jewelry, and other valuables. Did they just drop them anywhere? He didn't see any markers. Regardless, it wouldn't take him long to find some. How deep could the bogs be? He'd collect what treasure he could and head for the shore. He'd seen it clearly from the top of Mis's Mountain. He could reach there in no time and pay for passage across the sea. With luck he could make it back home by tomorrow or the next day.

Blinded by the angle of the sunlight, he shielded his face with one hand. With longer shadows and less light, the bogs became more difficult to navigate. The torches, still some distance away, hadn't moved much, if at all. He wanted to cling to hope but . . . the sun . . . had it reached the horizon? No, a sliver of sky remained between the earth and the sun. Didn't it? *Please, Je . . .*

He'd almost said it, the name of the Lord, but why should he call out to God in desperation if he hadn't believed in Him all along? If God existed, if God cared . . .

The patch of moss Magonus leaped to had only been a reflection, he discovered too late. His foot splashed down, taking his entire body with it into a shock of icy water. Cold, mucky water in his eyes, nose, and mouth. He'd thrown his hands out as he fell, and now they slapped down a short distance under the surface of the water to slimy earth. No . . . not earth. One hand pushed against something fleshy and—limb-like. At the same moment, something else emerged, as if his hand had become a fulcrum pushing it up. The *something*—it flopped onto

Magonus' back.

Mortified and gagging at the thought of what he touched, of what touched him, he scrabbled away from it. Water dribbled into his mouth and eyes, everything around him a blur of light and shadows. Heart racing. Nausea rising. Groping for solid earth and fearful of any more discoveries, he crawled on hands and knees, forcing his body through the frigid water. Unable to see clearly through blurry eyes and his own splashing, he struggled to get away from the thing. To get back on solid land.

With nothing to grab onto, he tried getting one foot under him. His foot got tangled in his cape and once free, slid in the muck. His body slid too. A tingling sensation, sheer panic, raced through him as he slipped—out of control—into a deeper pool in the bogs, and his head went under water.

He forced his eyes open. Something pale and stringy danced past his face. The failing light revealed little else in his sickly greenish surroundings.

Kicking, thrashing, groping—something brushed his legs, like fingers on a hand. A hand wanting to take hold of him and draw him down, down, down. How deep did this pool go?

Must get out! Need air—

A burst of air escaped his lungs, creating bubbles and a panicked urge to draw a breath. Hold it, hold it—can't breathe water—

Lord, save me . . . My God, help me . . .

Time stopped and blackness fell. Then light, so dazzling

bright, yet not blinding. So close to him. So warm. So loving. So terrifying!

The light pierced his mind and soul, illuminating something he'd ignored for so long. His conscience. The sins of his past, every consequential and inconsequential one surfaced in his mind, and then his deepest secret, something he'd done one day—rather, in one short hour.

Gripping a lantern and the box he'd picked up at the market, Magonus traipsed through the darkening woods toward an emerald green clearing. Toward a little shrine built in honor of some beloved god or goddess; he'd never had the courage to ask which one, but many he knew turned to this deity to obtain favors.

As he emerged from the trees, his gaze riveted to the knee-high carved stone altar and the single tree in the middle of the clearing. A shudder ran through him.

What was he doing? Should an argument with his father matter that much? So what if he didn't get his way? Did he really want to ask the help of some pagan god? He'd never taken the gods and goddesses seriously before.

Traces of previous offerings stained the flat top of the altar, a rectangular pillar covered on all sides with carvings of snakes or some such things. Sooty remnants of offerings littered the ground around it, along with spent candles and crusty dishes.

Magonus lifted the lid of his box and took a deep breath, a strong perfumed scent tickling his nose. He'd spent quite a bit of money on the stick of incense. And for what? Should he do this? What did he really believe?

He'd prayed with his parents to the Christian God, mouthing the words and going through the motions but never believing. He'd never understood the teaching about the Blessed Trinity, the Three Persons in One God. Besides, many of his friends prayed to these other gods. Did it matter one way or the other? Who was to say that one belief was right and the other wrong?

Magonus would put it to the test. If he got what he asked for . . .

Standing beneath the solitary tree, he touched the incense to the flame in the lantern he carried and stepped forward. Smoke trailed upward, along with his prayer, as he set the stick of incense on the altar. Discomfort niggled him somewhere inside, but he pushed it away and finished his prayer.

In the presence of the warm light, deep sorrow welled up inside Magonus. There was no god but God alone. Father, Son, and Holy Ghost. Somewhere deep inside, he'd known it all along.

Repenting of all his sins, warmth enveloped him. Christ above him. Christ below him. Christ on his left and on his right, ever so near to him, never giving up on him.

As unexpectedly as it had come, the brightness faded. Murky green light flooded his senses. His lungs screamed for air. Thrashing, groping, struggling . . . he didn't want to die.

As he whipped about, he stirred up stringy things and bumped unknown things, and an object landed in his palm, causing him to curl his fingers around it.

I deserve to die, but please, Lord . . .

Solid arms snaked around him from behind, gripped him hard, and hoisted him from the water, freeing him from the pool and reminding him of the moment he'd been deprived of his freedom by the Irish pirate on the coast of Roman Briton.

Magonus was thrown to the ground. Landing hard on his back, water rushed up his throat and spluttered from his mouth and nose. Shivering from the cold, he coughed hard, over and over, before opening his eyes.

His gaze shifted first to the object that had come to him in the bog. An odd-shaped greenish rock lay in his palm, its unusual shape giving him pause. It resembled a three-leaf clover. Had someone carved it to look this way? Something about it stirred his heart and made him think of—yes, that was it. It made him think of God and the Trinity that he had always found so hard to understand. Father, Son, and Holy Ghost.

He believed. He really truly believed!

Warmth flooded him, despite his wet clothes and the cool breeze whistling through the moss around him.

"Are you all right?"

A familiar face . . . Cillian knelt over him, dripping wet and panting hard. "What are you doing out here?"

His original intent shooting to the front of his mind, he grabbed Cillian by the arms and tugged himself upright. His soaked clothes fought against him, trying to weigh him down. "Tag, did you rescue him? Where is he? It's not too late—"

The golden sun melted into the horizon, half of it

hidden behind distant hills.

Head down and wet strands of hair in his face, Cillian helped Magonus to his feet. "It is too late," he whispered, his voice heavy with grief. "I couldn't find them at first, then I got there just as the horn blew. There was nothing that I could do." He dragged the back of his hand over his eyes and turned away. "We must go. Hurry. They've started back this way."

Stunned and struggling to accept Cillian's news, Magonus looked to where he'd last seen the druids. They'd gone from that spot, but he soon saw their torches, bigger and brighter now. And closer.

"Come!" Cillian tugged the wet sleeve of Magonus' tunic.

Feeling a closeness to Jesus, Magonus glanced at the special stone once more. Surrendering and trusting that God allowed all this for a reason, Magonus followed Cillian. He pulled his wet cape tighter around him as he leaped over little pools and rivulets and raced down strips of solid moss-covered earth.

Magonus could've died today too. Without faith.

Had Tag been given an opportunity to see God and to see his own soul? Had he been given a chance to repent of his sins and choose the one, true God?

"Come, now we can run." Cillian followed the last strip of land at the edge of the bog that met up with the muddy trail.

Shivering uncontrollably from the cool autumn air and his wet clothes, Magonus forced one step after the other, willing his body to run and keep up.

He could not let the gift of God go to waste. He must share this treasure with others. Starting today. He would have to share this Good News with Cillian and Rhona and everyone else who would listen to him. But how to explain it?

Magonus gripped the clover-shaped stone as he hurried after Cillian. He would live by faith and pray to know God better. He would not try to escape—as he'd longed to do every day since he'd arrived in Ireland.

He would offer his life as a shepherd to God to make up for the sins of his past. It wouldn't be enough, couldn't be enough to make amends to an all holy, almighty God. But he would unite it to the one sacrifice that mattered: the sacrifice of the Son of God for the salvation of the world.

Sorrow at losing his friend settled in his soul, and he vowed to let it remain there to remind him of the shortness of life and the urgency of spreading the Gospel. Supernatural joy accompanied the sorrow.

He was loved by the Almighty One, the only God, the Blessed Trinity: Father, Son, and Holy Ghost. As in the depths of the bog, he felt the Lord near him, behind and before him, beside and above him. And a prayer began to form in his mind.

Five-and-a-half years later . . .

Humming the little prayer that he'd made up about Christ's presence all around him, Magonus traipsed the rolling countryside on his way to the northern shore. He could already smell the salty air, and he imagined he heard waves crashing to the shore, but it could've been the wind racing over the rugged terrain. He had perhaps an hour or so left of what he'd estimated would be a ten-hour journey.

He would miss Cillian and Rhona. Not wanting to delay, he'd told no one of his pre-dawn departure, and he'd had nothing to leave as a gift except the little prayer he'd made up. By the light of the moon, he'd carved it into dirt at the foot of Mis's Mountain, near what had become their meeting place.

They wouldn't be happy, but he'd had to set off immediately. An angel had appeared to him in a dream. "Very soon you will return to your native country. Make for the northern shore," the heavenly entity had said. "It is time for your escape." And while he'd once longed for escape more than anything, Magonus now only wanted to follow the will of God. Since God had commanded him through an angel, he did not want to delay.

He'd miss the sheep and goats too. After spending all these years with them, the poor little beasts had come to feel like family. But he'd guided them toward a grassy field near Milchu's ring fort so someone would soon realize the flock had no shepherd.

Magonus took a deep breath of cool, fresh air and soaked in the beauty of the rolling green landscape. Over the past few years, he'd grown to love Ireland. Here, in this pagan land, he'd found the one, true God. Ever since his "baptism in the bogs," he'd spent hours every day in prayer, coming to know and love his Savior. He'd worked and fasted without complaining, accepting it all with trust and surrender.

His fate made sense to him now. His kidnapping and slavery had been punishment for his intentional lack of faith, a consequence of his ignoring the treasure offered to him from his childhood. Punishment, but also grace. A wake-up call. For he deserved death and hell because of his sins, but God had mercy on him.

With the help of Cillian and Rhona, he'd also learned the Celtic language, which allowed him to tell others about God. A few had even nicknamed him "holy boy," much to Milchu's disgust. The druid never wanted to hear about it. He already knew something of Christianity, divined it he'd said, and he stood in firm opposition of it coming to these lands.

Through prayer and contemplation during his lonely days tending sheep, Magonus had come to understand the pagan Irish a bit. All people were made for a relationship with the one, true God. Without God's revelation, the pagans floundered and hungered and created their own gods. But while these false gods required human sacrifice, the one true God took on human form and became the sacrifice Himself.

These people did not have the truth, but they were a religious people. If only they knew. He'd tried to teach them, but he just didn't have the words that could make sense to them.

"Like Lugus who has three faces?" Cillian asked after Magonus tried explaining the Holy Trinity.

"What? No, no, no. Not at all like that." Magonus shook his head adamantly.

"Oh, more like the goddess Morrigan," Rhona said. "She can manifest as a crow, a wolf, or an eel."

"No, that's not right either." Frustration came out in his tone. "God is three distinct persons sharing one divine nature. I'm sorry I can't explain better than that. It's a mystery, and it's not like your pagan gods at all." He wished he'd paid better attention to his catechism lessons.

Lost in thoughts of the past, Magonus stubbed his toe on a cluster of rocks and tumbled to the ground. Something fell from his pocket and clattered against the rocks—the special stone that he'd found in the bogs years ago. He didn't want to lose that. It reminded him of his conversion. And with its unusual shape, the way it looked like a three-leaf clover, it reminded him of . . .

The clover—Magonus had seen the little plant every single day, led his sheep to pasture in fields of clover and never once thought . . . These pagans, so connected to nature, maybe nature could help them understand God!

He gazed at the stone, appreciating the play of sunlight on the variegated shades of green and brown. A three-leaf clover. Three separate leaves . . . Three separate and distinct persons: Father, Son, and Holy Ghost. One clover. One divine nature!

Why hadn't he thought of it sooner? Along with the

prayer drawn in the dirt, he should've left the stone with his friends.

Magonus climbed to his feet just as a seagull called out and soared overhead. A few more steps took him to where he could see the Irish Sea below the rocky plateau on which he stood. Oh so aware of the treasure he'd received in his enslavement, he gazed in awe at the deep blue waves and the ship still some distance out. The ship that would take him home.

Turning back the way he'd come, filling with hope and joy and a spirit of adventure, Magonus shouted, "I'll miss you, Cillian and Rhona. My dear flock. And you too, land of Ireland. If only I'd been able to teach you . . ."

Magonus glanced at the clover-shaped stone and then lifted his eyes to heaven. "Lord, you gave me this stone as a sign that You are with me always and to help me understand You better. I leave this stone here as a continual prayer that Cillian and Rhona, and all of Ireland, may come to know You, Oh Most Holy Trinity."

Gripping the stone in his fingers, he drew his arm back and using the force of his entire body, pitched the stone into the air. Praying for the conversion of Ireland, he turned toward the sea.

He considered what else the angel had said to him in his dream, but he did not understand.

"One day you will be known as Patrick, and you will shepherd once again."

###

Many details about Saint Patrick are uncertain, including the exact years of his birth and death and the specific land in which he grew up. Some believe his given name was Maewyn or Magonus and that he did not receive the name Patrick until his ordination. Fortunately, history and Catholic tradition help us develop a good picture of this courageous saint and provide us with his very own writings. When developing the storyline and character, the author referred to the saint's autobiographical work, now called *Saint Patrick's Confessio*. Saint Patrick was captured as a teenager by Irish pirates, likely the actual historical figure Niall of the Nine Hostages. He was then taken to Ireland as a slave to herd and tend sheep, possibly for a druid chieftain named Milchu. Saint Patrick believed that God allowed him to be taken into captivity in Ireland because, in his own words, he "had gone away from God and did not keep his commandments" (*Confessio*). His conversion takes place in Ireland, but the specific details surrounding it are not given in his writings, so the author has taken creative liberty and hopes that this story will touch many hearts and maybe even spark a deeper faith in the hearts of young people.

ABOUT THE AUTHOR

THERESA LINDEN is the author of award-winning Catholic fiction, including the West Brothers contemporary series and the Chasing Liberty dystopian trilogy. One of her great joys is to bring elements of faith to life through a story. She has more than a dozen published books, three of which won awards from the Catholic Press Association. Her short stories appear in several anthologies, including *Secrets: Visible & Invisible*, and *Gifts: Visible & Invisible*. Her articles and interviews can be found on various radio shows and in magazines, including EWTN's *The Good Fight*, *The National Catholic Register*, *Catholic Digest*, *Today's Catholic Teacher*, and *Catholic Mom*. Her books are featured online on *Catholic Teen Books*, *Catholic Reads*, *FORMED*, and *Virtue Works Media*. A wife, homeschooling mom, and Secular Franciscan, she resides in northeast Ohio with her husband and children. You can learn more about her at www.TheresaLinden.com

Several Centuries Later, Ireland

A SINGLE DAY ... OR NOT

by Susan Peek

Staring intently at the open book on his lap, sixteen-year-old Brother Dearmad rubbed the back of his neck in growing frustration and heaved a sigh. As soon as the sound escaped into the quiet chapel, he cringed. Had the other monks heard him? How could they not have, crammed together in such a tiny space? Embarrassed, he looked up and cast a furtive glance around.

Whew. To his relief, his loud sigh didn't seem to attract any attention. The other brothers, squished in the limited number of choir stalls and practically spilling onto the floor, kept their eyes serenely closed. Their hands were hidden in the long flowing sleeves of their woolen black habits. They all seemed absorbed in heavenly contemplation, oblivious to being packed so tightly together.

Saint Patrick better give us a bigger church soon, Brother Dearmad thought wistfully, *or else stop inviting so many of us to the monastery.*

The weight of the heavy book on his lap nudged his thoughts back to that which had caused the embarrassing loud sigh in the first place: today's mysterious Scripture passage. He scratched his newly shaven head and lowered his gaze back to the page, wondering if any of the other monks wrestled with its meaning like he did. Was he the only one who found Latin such a nightmare to translate? The abbot, Father Darragh, always told him to be patient with himself. He was the youngest here, after all. Latin couldn't be learned in a day, Father said. In fact, nothing could. It would take years to master both the beautiful language of the Church and the perfection of religious life.

Brother Dearmad frowned. Father sure was right! At this rate, it would take him centuries to figure out this verse.

Despite the breathtaking beauty of the manuscript—which he knew was one of the monastery's greatest treasures—the delicately inscribed words on the page glared at him defiantly, stubbornly refusing to be translated by such a young monk. *Unus dies apud Dominum sicut mille anni, et mille anni sicut dies unus.* Hmm. What did that mean? He suspected this was going to bother him all day until he figured it out. Obviously it had something to do with a thousand years, *mille anni.* But what was that *dies unus* doing, tacked to the end of it? A single day? Ridiculous. How could a thousand years before God be the same as a single day? But that's what the passage, incredibly, seemed to claim. What on earth had Saint Peter been thinking when he wrote such an outlandish line in his epistle?

Brother Dearmad tried again to translate it, painstakingly applying the Latin that Father Darragh had patiently been attempting to teach him.

One day with the Lord is as a thousand years, and a thousand years as one day. That was what it seemed to be saying. It reminded him of one of the Psalms in the Divine Office that the monks chanted daily. *For a thousand years in Thy sight are as yesterday, which is past.* Well, obviously both King David and Saint Peter believed the same amazing thing. But how could this be? And why did it bother him so much that he didn't understand the meaning?

The tinkling of a bell, indicating the end of prayer, startled him and he nearly dropped the precious book. Flustered, he closed its fragile pages with a loud thump, the new sound making him wince. Would he ever learn to be quiet? Heat climbed up his neck. He placed the book on the bench beside him as carefully and silently as he could, then stood with the others. His elbow knocked against the arm of old Brother Oisin next to him, nearly toppling the ancient monk to the floor. Then his foot entangled with Brother Finn's leg. By now his whole face burned. Trying hard not to jostle or crash into anyone else, he filed outside with the others, who miraculously maintained perfect order and enviable calm as they exited the tiny chapel.

How many years would it take to make him a good monk? Two? Five? Twenty?

More like a hundred. No, make that two hundred. Same time I figure out Saint Peter's mysterious words. Discouragement tugged at Brother Dearmad's heart.

Saint Patrick, I want to be a worthy monk. I really do! Please help me!

Outside, a sharp breeze slapped his face, the salty ocean-smell tingling his nostrils. The rhythmic sound of waves crashing upon the distant shore filled his ears. A solitary brave seagull circled above them, being tugged this way and that by the currents of the strengthening wind. Brother Dearmad braced himself against the autumn chill, determined to offer the discomfort up to Jesus, to help Him save souls. To his relief, he managed to gather with the others around Father Darragh without tripping anyone. They quietly awaited instructions for the day's tasks.

A smile twitched at Father Darragh's lips, the way it always did when he was about to reveal a surprise to his sons. And a surprise it was, indeed!

"We have much work to do before winter," Father announced with a jolly wink. "Today we shall begin cutting logs, quarrying rocks, and collecting branches for the construction of our new church."

A new church! Before he could think, Brother Dearmad triumphantly shot a fist in the air and let out a whoop of excitement.

All eyes turned to him.

He froze with mortification.

Yep, two hundred years. At a minimum. He definitely needed a couple centuries to become a good monk. His heart sank in near-despair.

A carpet of orange and red leaves crinkled beneath his feet as Brother Dearmad tossed another branch onto the precariously balanced pile in the wheelbarrow. He paused to swipe his sleeve across his brow. Despite the cold air, sweat trickled down his face. His muscles ached, and his stomach yearned for a meal. The sun was already low on the horizon, a sinking golden orb in the western sky that took his breath away with its majestic beauty, yet offered zero warmth. He'd been sawing through low-hanging tree branches with his knife for hours, loading them into the creaky wooden barrow and wheeling it back and forth up the hill to the monastery yard all day. His brothers had long ago stopped. Their bodies were weaker, less robust than his, after decades of penance. He was only sixteen summers old, the youngest and fittest among them, so he'd asked Father Darragh permission to keep working until *Compline*, the Church's night prayer. This was the least he could do to prove his love for God and Saint Patrick.

Besides, the thought of someday raising a new church in this blessed corner of Ireland caused Brother Dearmad's heart to swell with happiness. Legends claimed that Saint Patrick himself had traversed this very hill when he'd headed to the northern shore, right before his escape back to Briton as a young man. The ground beneath Brother Dearmad's feet was, indeed, holy soil.

As he gazed towards the sea—drenched in pink and orange from the reflection of the sunset—he pictured future sailors, bone-weary upon the decks of their ships, spotting the church towering above the land, a beacon of hope and protection. What a magnificent sight that would be. Like a welcome to Ireland from Saint Patrick.

Brother Dearmad smiled as he imagined himself an elderly monk, stooped, fossilized and toothless, like ancient

Brother Oisin, surrounded by fresh-faced novices. *"I helped build this church,"* he would tell them proudly. *"It took us years."*

Years. The moment the word entered his mind, his memory flashed back to Saint Peter's mysterious Scripture passage, bringing with it the same twinge of confusion that he'd felt this morning. He'd forgotten about the verse until now. Oh, bother. Why did he have to remember it? Now it would probably bother him the rest of the day until he figured out its meaning. He mulled over the sentence in his head. *Unus dies apud Dominum sicut mille anni, et mille anni sicut dies unus. One day with the Lord is as a thousand years, and a thousand years as one day.*

Was his translation right? If so, what did it mean? Was Saint Peter saying that God could accomplish something in a single day that would normally take many years? Is that what King David had meant in the Psalm as well? Obviously God could do anything. But did He ever actually do that? He must, otherwise why would the Holy Ghost inspire both an apostle and a prophet to write about it?

A silly thought whizzed through Brother Dearmad's mind. Maybe God would fast-track his holiness. Make him a saint in one day. Wouldn't that be spectacular? He could stroll back to the monastery tonight with a halo. No more fumbling. No more blunders. No more mortifying reactions like shooting his fist in the air or sending anyone sprawling in the chapel. Imagine that—God making him a perfect monk in the blink of an eye!

He chuckled out loud at the ridiculousness of such a

scenario. *All right, stop daydreaming and get back to work.*

Nonetheless, he crossed himself and shot a prayer to Heaven. "Saint Patrick, please help me understand that Scripture. And while you're at it, it really would be amazing to become a saint in a day." He hoped the prayer wasn't irreverent. Surely Saint Patrick would understand his impatient longing for holiness.

Anyhow, time to cut more branches. Tracing again the Sign of the Cross upon himself, he bent to his knees to retrieve his knife. He'd set it on the ground a moment earlier when he'd tossed the last branch onto the wheelbarrow.

He couldn't see it.

Anywhere.

What? How strange. He was sure he'd set it right beside him.

He patted the dead leaves at his feet, searching for the missing knife. It was nowhere to be seen.

Bewilderment mounting, his glance took in a wide circle around him. Where on earth was it? He started digging frantically through the leaves. Would Father Darragh be angry when he realized the knife was lost? He was the kindest priest Brother Dearmad had ever met, but still, the vow of poverty made everything in the monastery valuable. Father was always drilling into his monks that they must take care of the tools God so lovingly provided for them. Would Father kick him out of the monastery this time? Was this the last straw? How many stupid things was a novice allowed to do before finally being dismissed? He had to find the knife!

"Saint Patrick, please help me." He brushed the leaves away with rising panic. "Saint Patrick, Saint Patrick . . ."

His fingers touched something solid, half-buried in the dirt. Could it be the hilt? How would the knife have gotten buried? Frowning, Brother Dearmad dug at the object. No, it wasn't the knife. A splotchy green stone peeked out from under layers of dirt.

Curious, he gouged the little rock from the ground and placed it in his palm. It was caked in what looked like centuries of mud. He rubbed it between his fingers to clean it, noticing immediately its unusual shape. Speckled in several shades of green and crisscrossed with tiny veins of brown, it exactly resembled a three-leaf clover. The precise shape made him think that someone had carved it, yet the closer he looked, the more Brother Dearmad was sure it was natural. God Himself had fashioned this little stone into a perfect shamrock. Imagine that!

Brother Dearmad grinned. He couldn't wait to show the other monks this interesting little treasure. It would make everyone think of Saint Patrick. Shamrocks and the great saint were inseparable. Everybody knew that. Saint Patrick had used a three-leaf clover to explain the Holy Trinity to the Irish of his time. The two always went together.

Speaking of Saint Patrick, Brother Dearmad suddenly realized he'd been praying to him a mere moment ago. Did finding this shamrock have something to do with his prayer? Before he could even remember what he'd been praying for, an overwhelming sense of a heavenly presence gripped him. It was so strong that his heart started pounding fiercely.

Thankfully he was already on his knees, because at that moment an interior certainty of Saint Patrick standing invisibly before him flooded his entire being. He felt like he might die on the spot of joy. Saint Patrick was here, *right here*, unseen but more real than anything Brother Dearmad had ever experienced.

"Saint Patrick," he whispered in awe, "please ask God to make me a saint." The desperate words bubbled up from the depths of his heart. He squeezed the shamrock-shaped stone in his hand. The rock should have been cold, but it seemed to radiate warmth. The feel of it in his hand filled his heart with peace, making him certain that Saint Patrick had heard his prayer.

Then, as quickly as it had come, the tangible presence of Saint Patrick disappeared, leaving Brother Dearmad alone in the woods. Before sadness at the saint's departure had time to overcome him, another unexpected visitor appeared. A tiny bird swooped out of nowhere and landed on the ground in front of him. It started to chirp, making his heart instantly melt at the beauty of the sound. It was unlike any birdsong in Ireland. In fact, the bird itself was of a species Brother Dearmad had never seen before. Its feathers were so snowy white that they almost glowed. The bird hopped a few paces to the side, and that's when Brother Dearmad spotted the knife, innocuously lying on the ground right in front of him, as if it had been there all along.

The white bird looked up at Brother Dearmad and cocked its tiny head, as if watching to see what he would do next. Still dazed from the recent presence of Saint Patrick, Brother

Dearmad picked up the knife and wedged it into the belt around his habit. He must be careful not to lose it again . . . especially after the saint had returned it in such a stupefying manner! Yet Brother Dearmad sensed that Saint Patrick had come to him with more in mind than a misplaced knife. He gazed at the green stone in his palm and was suddenly sure, dead sure, that Saint Patrick himself had once touched this stone. For some reason, the saint was bequeathing it to him.

The bird hopped, as if to get his attention, and tweeted again. The sound took Brother Dearmad's breath away with its loveliness. So lulling was the bird's call that he felt he could listen to it for a lifetime and never grow tired of its sound. No harp in Ireland could match the graceful notes of that little bird's song!

Rising in the air, the bird fluttered its snowy wings, as if inviting him to follow it. Brother Dearmad got up from his knees and, clutching Saint Patrick's treasure tightly in his fist, walked behind the bird as it flitted from tree to tree. Its twittering and cheeping continued, warming his heart with its song. In fact, it warmed not only his heart, but his body as well. The autumn chill disappeared. The setting sun was suddenly party to the heavenly game, pouring its gentle rays down and flooding him with a delightful heat.

Oblivious to everything else, Brother Dearmad kept his eyes on his new little friend the bird as it led him playfully through the woods, enchanting him with its unearthly song and making him long for Heaven. The shamrock stone in his hand locked his thoughts on the Blessed Trinity, sparking a fire of love within him that seemed to burn deeper and hotter with every heartbeat.

He had no idea how long he followed the singing creature. He was vaguely aware of strange periods of darkness, which lasted the space of a few breaths, as if the sun had set for a moment or two, then rose again. Impossible, of course, but that was the impression that he got. Not that he was scrutinizing the sun. All his attention was riveted on the sweet little bird, its charming song, and the yearning for God expanding in his heart. How kind God was, to create such beauty! Clutching the shamrock stone now in a death grip, Brother Dearmad's soul soared with rapturous love for the Blessed Trinity. He wanted God so badly that it physically hurt.

Thank you, Saint Patrick, for whatever it was that you did back there. Thank you for this joy! Thank you for these graces!

After some time following the little bird, his heart started to hurt. Suddenly he was unable to walk any further for the pain of love crashing through him. He sat down on a boulder, the thought of God consuming him, making him feel like his insides would burst from love and longing.

Seeing him sit, the little white bird flapped its wings in what looked like a good-bye wave, then, before Brother Dearmad could object, his friend took flight. Higher and higher above the trees it climbed, until its diminutive body was lost from view in the puffy white clouds that floated through the bright blue sky.

Sadness tugged at Brother Dearmad's heart. But it was a sorrow mingled with unspeakable peace. Happiness even. He stared at the sky for a long time. But the bird did not come back.

It was only then that the color of the sky registered with him. Perfect blue.

What . . . wait! How could that be? It was evening, not day! Startled and disoriented, Brother Dearmad sprang to his feet and looked around. Shock jolted through him and his jaw dropped. Every tree stood blossom-laden, green branches decked in pink and white buds. His gaze shot to the ground. The carpet of dead leaves beneath his feet had somehow been replaced with verdant green grass. Wildflowers dotted the rolling hills as far as his eyes could see. His wheelbarrow, overflowing with branches, was nowhere in sight.

For a long moment, Brother Dearmad could only stand there, dumbstruck, his heart beating wildly with a mixture of pain and surprise. He shook his head, trying to clear his thoughts. Was he dreaming? Was he losing his mind? He had to get back to the monastery and tell Father Darragh everything. Maybe he was going insane! Surely the holy abbot would be able to discern what was going on.

Gripping the shamrock stone in his hand, he started walking uphill in the direction of the monastery as fast as he could. A strange urgency clutched him and his pace quickened to a jog, then a run. His chest felt like it was expanding, as if his heart was doubling, then tripling, in size. Sweet fire burned his insides. God was near, so near!

He had to reach Father Darragh! Something strange was happening to his heart! It was growing. On fire. He was being consumed with love! He was going to die!

He ran quicker and quicker, hardly able to breathe. As his

feet flew over the ground, he couldn't believe his eyes at how overgrown the hilly path had become. Bushes that hadn't existed mere hours ago had somehow sprouted and grown to full-size. In the valley below, a sprawling orchard stretched out before him that wasn't there this morning. Strange new ships dotted the sea. He noticed a barn that had miraculously been built in the time he'd been cutting branches. What on earth was going on? How had the monks managed to. . . . He reached the top of the hill and stopped dead in his tracks.

A magnificent church, with its spire reaching towards Heaven, filled the place where an empty field near the monastery had once been. Brother Dearmad's eyes bulged.

He swallowed and transferred Saint Patrick's treasure from hand to hand so he could wipe the sweat from his palms. His heart galloped, his whole body blazing with an inferno of love. Resisting the urge to run the rest of the way, he composed himself, like a good monk would, and slowly walked towards the building he vaguely recognized as his monastery. Surely this was all just a strange dream?

A monk outside with a hoe must have spotted him, for the man raised a hand in a friendly greeting. He set down the hoe and started walking towards Brother Dearmad. His tonsured hair was gray, his face wrinkled. Brother Dearmad didn't recognize him, which was odd because of course he knew all his brothers. Perhaps this old monk was visiting. Yet how strange that Father Darragh would hand a visitor a hoe and put him to work. Especially someone as elderly as the monk approaching him.

"Greetings in Christ, my friend." The strange monk reached him. They embraced with the customary monastic gesture of welcome. Then the old monk looked Brother Dearmad up and down with obvious bewilderment. "You are very young, yet I see you wear the habit of our holy order. Welcome, welcome. Are you alone? Do you seek lodging? Have you come from afar?"

The questions left Brother Dearmad speechless.

When he didn't answer, the old monk introduced himself. "I'm Brother Sean." He winked. "I used to be the guest master here, but Father Cian retired me to pasture a few months ago. Come, my young brother. Let me take you to him. He's our abbot. He will welcome you to our guesthouse."

Tingles ran up and down Brother Dearmad's spine. He found his voice, though it came out high and squeaky. "Father . . . *Cian*? What? Who? Father Darragh is our abbot! And Brother Tadhig is our guest master. Who—who are you? There's no Brother Sean here!"

This whole conversation was incredible. Impossible. None of this could be happening!

The old monk's eyebrows lifted in bewildered surprise. "Father Darragh? No, I'm sorry. Our abbot is Father Cian. He's held the office for fifty years. I know that for a fact, because I entered the year he was elected."

By now Brother Dearmad's heart was so inflamed that he thought his whole body was on fire.

Brother Sean stroked the gray stubble on his chin. "The previous abbot was Father Senan. And before him, Father

Liam. Of course they've both passed to their reward now. I've been here since my nineteenth year and never heard the name Father Darragh."

Dizziness threatened to knock Brother Dearmad to the ground. He desperately rubbed the shamrock stone between his fingers. *Saint Patrick, what on earth did you do to me?*

No sooner had the prayer entered his mind than understanding flooded him and his heart leapt with explosive love for God. *Unus dies apud Dominum sicut mille anni, et mille anni sicut dies unus.* The incredible words ran through his head. *One day with the Lord is as a thousand years, and a thousand years as one day.*

And suddenly, Brother Dearmad *knew.*

Brother Sean's kind eyes filled with worry and he put a steadying hand on Brother Dearmad's arm. "Are you alright, Brother? Come, sit down. You've turned awfully pale."

"It's because I'm going to die today."

The words just came. Brother Dearmad hadn't thought them, hadn't called them forth from his lips. But the second they were uttered, he knew he'd spoken truth.

Without warning, weariness overtook his body. Fatigue unlike any he'd known before. He could hardly remain standing. He leaned on Brother Sean and let him help him the rest of the way to the monastery. By the time they reached the door and stumbled inside, he was so weak he could no longer place one foot in front of the other. Everything inside him was withering, life fast ebbing away with every struggling breath he drew. Yet unbounded peace and joy were sweeping him away in their torrent. How he loved God! Charity burned through him. He was dying of love!

He collapsed on the floor.

Brother Sean dropped to his knees beside him, his expression a mask of confusion and helplessness.

"Brother Sean, fetch a priest. Please." He gasped for breath. His voice was strained, a mere whisper. "I'd like to pronounce my holy vows and confess before I die."

Alarm flicked across the old monk's face. He called out to another monk in the corridor, and the brother rushed over. He wore a traveling cape and carried a basket. It looked as if he was about to leave on a journey.

"I'm a priest." He quickly set the basket on the floor, whipped off his cape, and within seconds was hearing Brother Dearmad's confession.

From the depths of the monastery, more and more monks appeared. He recognized none of them. Someone handed holy oils to the priest for Extreme Unction. The brothers surrounded him, all eager to help, their expressions grave, their voices comforting. After the anointing, Brother Dearmad pronounced his blessed vows of poverty, chastity, and obedience. His happiness was unbearable. His heart could no longer contain such transports of joy.

A cup of water touched his lips. A blanket spread its warmth over him. And the entire time, he yearned only to fly to God.

"What is your name?" the priest gently asked. "From what monastery do you hail, that we may send word to your abbot?"

"I am Brother Dearmad. This is my monastery."

The monks stared at him, uncomprehending.

"I went to cut wood for the new church. The church you already built. I . . . I don't know what happened."

Stunned silence.

Then one monk whispered, "Brother *Dearmad*, you say?"

"Yes."

"We . . . we heard about you." The monk's jaw dropped and he blurted to the others, "The legend! Remember?" His gaze encompassed the circle of monks. "A young brother named Dearmad, back in the early years of our monastery, before the church was built. He disappeared into the woods and was never seen again."

A collective gasp erupted from the group.

Someone said, "This church was built two hundred years ago!"

A wave of shock rippled through the room.

Brother Dearmad could hardly believe his ears. *Two hundred years?*

TWO HUNDRED YEARS?!

And yet, deep down, he knew it was true. He could almost hear Saint Patrick chuckling.

"What day," Brother Dearmad asked, "is it?"

"Do you not know? 'Tis the seventeenth of March, the feast of Saint Patrick."

Brother Dearmad could not help it. He laughed for joy. Soon, oh so soon, he would be with the beloved saint who had shown him that, indeed, one day with the Lord is as a thousand years, and a thousand years as one day.

He smiled and his eyes fell on the traveling basket that the priest had hastily set down on the floor. "Good Father, where are you journeying?"

"Across the sea to Briton, my son."

Briton. The land of Saint Patrick's birth. The land to which he'd escaped after being a slave in Ireland. Had the saint left the green stone for someone else to find, before continuing to the shore to make his escape? Had the shamrock, carved by God, lain buried in the dirt for centuries, waiting for Brother Dearmad to unearth it?

He would never know for sure. But a grin twitched his lips as he imagined the legends that might spring up around the blessed object.

With his last ounce of strength, Brother Dearmad lifted his hand and placed the shamrock stone into the basket. It was only right that Saint Patrick's treasure should follow in his footsteps to Briton, where, Brother Dearmad prayed, great graces would flow to others who found it.

"Father, take this with you to Briton," he begged.

"Why? What is it, my son?"

Brother Dearmad smiled. "Let's just say it's a treasure from Saint Patrick."

He could see by their faces that his brothers wanted more of an explanation. But he could not give it, for his time was up.

Peacefully Brother Dearmad closed his eyes and fell asleep in the Lord.

###

This story is adapted from an ancient legend of an unknown Irish saint. As his name is recorded nowhere in history, I have named him Dearmad, which in Gaelic means Forgotten.

ABOUT THE AUTHOR

SUSAN PEEK is a wife, mother, grandmother, Third Order Franciscan, and bestselling Catholic novelist. Her passion is writing stories of little-known saints and heroes. All her young adult novels have been awarded the coveted Catholic Writers Guild Seal of Approval and are implemented into Catholic school curricula not only across the nation, but in Canada, Australia, and New Zealand as well. *Saint Magnus the Last Viking* and *The King's Prey: Saint Dymphna of Ireland* were both Amazon #1 Sellers among Catholic books. *The King's Prey* was also voted one of *Catholic Reads* TOP 10 BEST CATHOLIC BOOKS OF 2017 and was a Finalist for the 2018 Catholic Arts and Letters Award. *Crusader King* was featured as one of the 50 Most Popular Catholic Homeschooling Books in 2013. Susan lives in northeastern Kansas, where she can usually be found with her nose in a book, researching obscure saints to write about. Visit her at www.SusanPeekAuthor.com.

12th Century, England

LUCY AND THE HIDDEN CLOVER

by Antony B. Kolenc

"Sister Brigitte might die today, Lucy."

That's what Sister Regina told me in a whispered voice this morning after *Prime*, the prayers at dawn sung by the black nuns of Harwood Abbey.

Poor Sister Brigitte is one of the dearest nuns to the novices and to us other girls who live at this convent. She was so weak during January that she predicted 1185 would be her final year in this world. Then she recovered in February, only to take ill again this month, just before Lent began. Last night, she got such a hot fever that Sister Regina doesn't expect her to survive this day. If she dies, maybe Mother Abbess will place the convent into mourning.

"May I go and pray with her?" I ask. Sister Regina is in charge of all us younger girls—orphans and girls like me, left here by Father almost a year ago while he journeys for a time with our manor lord.

"Of course you may," Sister Regina says. She tucks a stubborn strand of golden hair under the tight cloth that runs across her pale forehead, around her cheeks, and along the bottom of her chin. Now her pretty face is entirely framed in white, below the thick black veil that flows over her head and shoulders.

If I ever become a nun, I'll have willful hairs too, except mine will be even more noticeable because they're so dark and my hair is so difficult to comb. Who knows if I'll ever find out, or even if I'll have a choice? At only twelve years of age, I still have two years before Father decides what is to become of me—whether I shall marry or be sent off to a convent as a novice.

I adjust my belt so that my white tunic doesn't drag across the floor while I walk to Sister Brigitte's cell. As I near, her wheezing spills into the hallway. I knock on her door and wait a moment before entering. There she is, shivering under her covers, with her black habit folded on the little wooden chair by her bed. I've never seen her without her veil, her shorn gray hair covered only by a bed cap. That would be one of the hardest parts about becoming a novice: having my black hair bunched up and cut down with a sharp blade—a symbol of a novice's new life in Christ.

"Lucy . . . my dear," Sister Brigitte says, her eyes slitting open.

I take her frail, burning hand into my own and squeeze it gently. "I came to pray with you."

She can barely press my hand back, but she smiles and

closes her eyelids while I pray aloud. Wetness fills the corners of her eyes as her lips move silently with my voice. When I finish, she looks at me again.

"You are . . . kind," she says, each word a mighty labor. "Are you . . . happy here?"

I nod. "All the nuns have been so kind to me this past year."

She gets a faraway look. "My father . . . forced me to come . . . to this convent . . . when I was but . . . a few years older than you. It took . . . a long time before . . . I was happy . . . in this life."

That sounds impossible: Sister Brigitte is one of the holiest, most joyful nuns I've ever met.

"Is there anything I can get for you?" I say. "A sip of water?"

She sticks her skinny elbows into the wool-stuffed mattress and props up her body a few inches, trying to look me in the eye. "Will you . . . help me?"

"Of course, anything."

"Will you find . . . the hidden clover?" She falls back on the mattress in an exhausted heap.

We younger girls often spend time in the meadow, searching through patches of clover to find one with four leaves instead of three. Some say that three-leaf clovers are a symbol of God—the Trinity of Father, Son, and Holy Ghost. The four-leaf ones are extra special because they're so rare and difficult to find. Perhaps that's what Sister Brigitte means by the *hidden clover*. Except this winter has been harsh, and the fields of clover won't come for over a month. She must have forgotten that in her illness.

"There are no clovers to find yet, Sister. 'Tis only March. I'm sorry."

A tear streams down her cheek. "'Tis . . . our . . . only chance . . . for healing."

Whose healing does she mean—hers and who else's? Maybe clovers have secret curing properties. "I can send for Brother Lucius, the healer," I say.

"Nay." Her eyelids battle to stay open. "Just find . . . the clover."

"I don't understand, Sister. What clover?" Maybe she means something else. "Where is it?"

"The cave." She chokes up a mouthful of sickness and spits it into a cloth. "Hidden in . . . the cave."

A clover growing in a cave?

She coughs again. "A dragon . . . guards . . . its hiding place."

On Sundays just like this one, Father used to tell me and my brothers stories about dragons as we'd peer up from the grassy field at clouds shaped like dragons and other flying creatures. But Sister Brigitte must be having delusions. Surely we would know if a dragon were living in a nearby cave.

"What is this clover used for?" I ask.

"'Twill bring . . . us . . . peace."

Her eyes stay closed a while, 'til it seems she's become unconscious. Her breathing gets smoother, but her throat wheezes. She may have fainted due to the fever. Then her eyes pop open and she turns to me. "*Please* . . . find the clover," she mutters, before falling back into a fevered sleep.

I'm not sure how to help Sister Brigitte, but later in the morning a tap comes on the convent door. Sister Regina answers it. 'Tis Father Clement, the abbey's prior. He says he's here to receive Sister Brigitte's last Confession. Her death truly must be near if he's here for that.

He enters without even a smile on his bearded face, so serious in his black robe. Though monks often look somber during this long season of Lent, today is a Sunday—a time to celebrate our Lord's Resurrection. The prior's sadness must be due to Sister Brigitte's illness.

"Lucy," Father Clement says when he spots me, finally a smile on his lips. "I am glad to see you."

I greet him. His presence here may be a sign from God that I should try to find this healing clover. I don't understand many things in this world, but Father Clement is a learned monk, and he's standing alone with me while Sister Regina goes to fetch Sister Cecilia.

"Prior," I say. "Do you know anything about a cave in these parts?"

He touches his thumb and finger to his beard and tugs on it. "Do you mean the old storage cave up the eastern abbey trail?" I know which trail he means. Unfortunately, he doesn't know anything about a hidden clover when I ask him about that. He gives me a suspicious look, but before he can inquire, the two nuns return to escort him to Sister Brigitte's cell.

The novice girls need special permission to do anything around here, but we younger girls have a bit more freedom. I don't know any rule that would stop me from walking on abbey grounds during my free time before Mass. So, while the prior and nuns head down the hall, I hurry to the supply room and get the fire-making kit and lamp. I've never been to this cave and have no idea how dark 'twill be inside.

I slip out the front door, leaving the stone convent behind me. Then I follow the thin path of the eastern trail into the barren woods and up a hill, being careful not to get too much mud on my leather shoes. If I soil my tunic, Sister Cecilia—the sternest obedientiary at the convent—will give me double chores tomorrow as a penance. Maybe she'll be understanding, though, because I'm only trying to carry out the wishes of a dying nun. Imagine if I find a healing clover that can be used to break that fever!

The cave is farther into the woodland than I realized. Sister Regina says that we girls should travel in pairs to stay safe outdoors. I would have asked Maud to come along, except she's so loud and boisterous, and I'm not sure whether this quest is something that might get me into trouble in the end. I hope not.

I keep climbing the steep slope. How sad that Sister Brigitte was forced to come to this abbey. I've heard stories about other girls who didn't want to become nuns, either. Yet God works in mysterious ways. How long did it take Sister Brigitte to find her happiness here, I wonder. What finally touched her heart?

Pale edges of jagged stone arise near the top of the hill. *The cave.* I light the lamp and thaw my hands with my breath in the winter chill. The vigorous journey has kept most of my body warm—except for my nose, cheeks, and hands, that is. The cave is dark, indeed; 'tis a good thing I brought a lamp.

The air inside stinks like the thick odor from Sister Angelica's bean soup when she leaves it burning over the fire. Do serpents live in caves? Maybe that's what Sister Brigitte means by a dragon. Luckily, 'tis still too cold for poisonous adders to be awake. I pick up a branch to defend myself, just in case.

The cave has a broad entrance that opens into a wide room. The lamplight reveals a narrow passage that continues into the black depths. I hope the clover isn't down *there*. I can see why Father Clement called this a storage cave—there are bits of old wooden crates strewn about, and the remains of broken items that must have been kept here long ago when the abbey was still too small to store all its supplies.

Where would a clover grow in a cave like this in the middle of March? *Nowhere, that's where.* Either Sister Brigitte has entirely lost her senses or else that clover isn't a living thing.

I hold the lamp up and wander the stone room, poking with my stick at debris along the floor. No sign of a clover. I get closer to the walls. The stones are uneven, with dozens of crevices. Maybe the clover is stuck inside one of those.

There! Writing carved into the wall—the letters *B* and *L*, along with the word *amor*. I'm not perfect with reading Latin, but I think that word means *love*—not God's love, but human love. Under the words is a drawing. I hold the lamp closer to make out what it might be.

Oh my! A black thing suddenly moves on the wall near my raised hand. It wriggles and turns away from the light. The entire wall seems to be squirming in the lamplight. *'Tis alive!*

I fall back a step. There's a bat sleeping in the crevice near the drawing carved into the stone, and bats all over the cave wall, nestled into cracks. I move the light away, and the bats settle back to rest.

"This is addle-pated," I whisper to myself and the little bat. "You shouldn't have come here, Lucy."

I make the Sign of the Cross and pray for the help of the saints to either show me this hidden clover or give me enough sense to get out of here before my long, black hair and tunic are covered in bats. Sister Cecilia would give me extra chores for a week if I came back with my clothes torn apart by little teeth and claws.

Except I can't leave yet. Poor Sister Brigitte might die today, and a few sleepy bats shouldn't stop me from finding that clover for her. This isn't the first mystery I've had to solve. Nor is it the first time I've walked into danger in the dark. Plus, I got a closer look at that drawing when I moved the lamp away: a carving of some kind of creature. Maybe that clover is hidden under one of the sleeping bats.

With my palm shielding the light from the bats, I draw

near to the carving—a dragon, actually. So that's what Sister Brigitte meant. Below the drawing is another crevice, too small for a bat. Could the clover be inside there? And what else: a spider or beetle or creepy-crawling creature?

For the love of Sister Brigitte, I hold my breath and stick my hand into the crevice. My fingers touch something: a small stone—rough, but not like the cave wall. There's a string attached to it, a thin strip of twine, maybe. I grab it and slip my hand from the crack. Then I step away and hold it up to the lamp.

The hidden clover!

'Tis small enough to fit in my palm. Naturally shaped like a three-leaf clover, its speckled green-brown surface barely reflects the light. The piece of twine threaded through a hole in the stone is broken and frayed at both ends, but it seems to have been a necklace at one time. How long has it been in this cave, and how did it get here? Sister Brigitte may have hidden it decades ago for some strange reason.

The bats squirm along the wall again. One of them stretches a wing.

Time to go.

I head out of the cave into the morning light and hasten down the trail. I need to get this clover back to the convent before I'm late for Mass. Maybe 'twill bring the healing and peace that Sister Brigitte desires.

Sister Brigitte is in a heavy sleep when I arrive back to her cell after our Mass in the convent chapel. On special

Sundays, we sometimes celebrate Mass with the monks in the main abbey church, but not today.

"Sister Brigitte," I say, touching her arm still hot with fever. "'Tis Lucy. I've returned. I found it."

I take out the green stone. How odd that this rock is in the shape of a three-leaf clover. 'Tis far too coarse a stone to have been fashioned that way by any man. A stone-crafter would have smoothed its roughness and carved its edges into more pronounced sides. Nay, this stone was made by nature.

Also, there is something familiar about the rough shape of this stone. I've seen it before somewhere, I'm certain. Not the stone itself; nothing as clear as that. I wish I could remember.

Sister Brigitte still isn't stirring, though her breathing is smooth and deep. I need her to wake up, if only for a little while. I have a score of questions. Why did she hide the clover in that cave? Why did she draw a dragon, which can be a symbol of the devil? How can the clover bring healing, and for whom? Many, many questions, but she doesn't revive to answer even one of them. I leave her resting in her cell.

I shuffle down the empty hallway, gliding my fingertips along its blank stone walls. I need to find out what those letters mean—the *B* and *L* and *amor*. The Latin word *amor* is not usually the term used to describe God's love for us; 'tis often a word a woman uses about the man she loves. That makes me wonder even more why this clover holds such great value for Sister Brigitte.

I arrive in the vestibule near the front door, where Sister Cecilia is piling brown blankets on the floor. Maybe I should tell her about the clover and the cave; I don't want to be punished for keeping secrets about Sister Brigitte. Mother Abbess insists on knowing everything that goes on with the nuns in this convent.

I need time to walk and think. "Is that a delivery for the monks?" I ask, as I glance to the floor.

She points to the pile. Her slender fingers are the longest I've ever seen, but they look normal on a woman of such towering height. "Aye, Lucy. Would you run those blankets to the boys' dormitory for me?"

I gather the blankets into my arms and head out the door. This delivery gives me the perfect reason to get out into the brisk air and walk again. I don't have to break a single rule to do so, either. Maybe I'll see my best friend Xan along the way. He's amazing at solving mysteries and would undoubtedly help me.

I head up the lane toward the dorm, working through the clues. Surely the *B* on the cave wall stands for *Brigitte*. If that is so, then the *L* must also be a name—maybe a man's name. Could it be that Sister Brigitte fell in love before she came to this convent? Maybe her father forced her to leave a love behind at her manor. Nuns give up worldly love for men and exchange it for a heavenly love for Jesus. They promise to stay chaste and disavow human desires. Except Sister Brigitte was forced to come to this nunnery.

What can all these clues mean? Sister must have fallen

in love with a man at some time in her youth. This hidden clover has something to do with him. Maybe that's why she carved a dragon in the cave: a symbol of her despair or regret. She told me that this clover was *our* only chance for healing and that it could bring *us* peace. She was speaking as though this other person—this man—were still living. If so, then he must be someone nearby if this stone can still bring them healing today.

Someone nearby? I'm certain that Sister Brigitte's far-off manor is located west of York.

This man must be someone at the abbey—one of the servants or lay brothers, perhaps—or maybe someone from Penwood or Oakwood Manors.

How many men do I know here who have names that begin with an *L*? Leonard, the lay brother who works in the refectory; Brother Lucius, the leech; Brother Leo, the mean monk who always yells at the boys in the dormitory; Liam, the servant who sometimes works with Xan in the granges.

Who else? I don't know every one of them.

As I near the dorm, the din of boys playing Sunday games in the meadow echoes toward me.

"Lucy!" Little Joshua comes running down the lane. He must have spotted me from the top of the meadow with his sharp eyes. He's one of my favorite boys here because of his kind and giving heart. If Joshua is around, then Xan must be nearby too. The pair of them often travel together.

Joshua skids to a stop in front of me, as I put my hand to my forehead and peer up the hill.

"Are you looking for Xan?" he says. "He's in the library, studying."

Of course he is. He's often there ever since Brother Andrew began teaching him to read and write.

Joshua walks with me toward the boys' dorm, laughing and telling a story about the game they're playing. The orphan boys work hard at the abbey, but they make up for it once they reach that meadow.

"Leave the girls alone, Joshua!" a gruff voice shouts from the upstairs window of the two-story, stone dorm—Brother Leo, of course, with his wrinkly face and wild gray eyebrows. He's often tasked with supervising the orphan boys.

Joshua breaks from my side immediately. "I have to go, Lucy. G'bye!"

That's how strict Brother Leo is. No one will ever forget the time he paddled John outside the boys' dormitory, directly in front of the other boys, yelling at John about discipline the whole time. He—

Nay, it cannot be!

I now remember where I've seen that odd-shaped clover. I once caught a glimpse of its rough outline sketched on a piece of parchment in the boys' dormitory. Actually, the parchment was being held by someone—Brother Leo. He was sitting on the steps of the dorm, staring at it while he prayed.

Surely that awful Brother Leo can't be the man who stole Sister Brigitte's heart! Of all the monks at the abbey, he's the very strictest, always lecturing the boys about penance and obedience to God.

What should I do? If I confront Brother Leo with my suspicions, what would I say? Knowing him, he would explode in a fit of anger and report me to Mother Abbess for a severe punishment.

But I can't ignore this. Sister Brigitte trusted me to find the hidden clover for her—to bring them healing and peace, she said. Maybe she would want me to take this stone to Brother Leo.

Trust God, Lucy. He always makes things right.

I deliver the pile of blankets to the bottom of the dormitory stairs, inside the open wooden door with the ringed, metal handle. Then I take out the green clover pendant from the pouch on my leather belt. I grasp the frayed twine and let it dangle.

Here I go. "Brother Leo?" I call up to him. "Might I speak with you a moment?"

He marches down the steps and rebukes a boy running past the dormitory entrance behind me. He seems offended that a girl lingers within the boys' dorm. He lifts a thick finger from under his black robe as though to reprimand me, but then his face goes blank with shock, turning to disbelief and even joy.

"What!" he says, rushing down to me. "Could it be?" He snatches the clover pendant out of my outstretched hand and holds it up to the daylight, laughing as he spins it around in his purply fingers. "My Lord, my Lord! After all these years, someone has finally found it. Praise be to the Lord and His saints for answering my prayers after these many years!"

Now I'm doubly confused. Did Sister Brigitte steal the pendant from this monk and hide it away from him? Why would she do that? Maybe I've been too hasty in judging Brother Leo.

"Where did you find this?" he says, folding his hefty fingers over the green rock as though it were a priceless treasure. "I have searched the woodland for almost forty years looking for this necklace. See?" He reaches into his pouch and pulls out a torn sketch of a clover—the same parchment I spied before.

"What is it?" I say.

He's still smiling; I've never seen him so happy. "A holy shamrock brought to these shores from Ireland. There are many legends about this stone, Lucy. Some say Saint Patrick found it while he was still a slave, while others say Patrick formed it in Heaven and sent it down as a sign of his intercession and of God's great love for us. But—"

Brother Leo nearly falls to the ground, leaning against the wall.

"Are you all right, Brother?"

He steadies himself. "Do you know the date today, Lucy?"

"Nay." I don't care much about dates, except for the date Father said he would return to get me.

Brother Leo laughs and can't seem to stop. "Today . . . is . . . the seventeenth of March!" He can barely speak through his gasps of joy. "'Tis the day of Saint Patrick's death! The Irish monks mark this day as a time of special blessing. And, lo, this is the very day you return to me the precious Shamrock of Saint Patrick. Do you not see the hand of God behind this wonder?"

Maybe Irish monks celebrate this date, but no one at the convent does. When Brother Leo smiles, the wrinkles on his face grow deeper yet somehow disappear. If he laughed this much all the time, he'd probably be the boys' favorite monk. It seems as if I've brought him more joy today than he's felt in forty years.

"This shamrock was given to me by my uncle, who was also a monk," he continues. "When I told him my decision to follow the way of Saint Benedict, he blessed me with it." His chapped fingers caress the rough edges of the green rock. "This stone has been passed from one generation of monks to the next for hundreds of years, Lucy—brought to England by the Irish monks before even my great-grandfather walked upon this earth. And in every generation, the legend of this stone's miraculous power grows."

Now what do I say? Maybe I should tell him that I found the necklace in the woodland. That would make this moment perfect, and he could go about his life believing only that the most amazing of miracles occurred on this seventeenth of March. He could remain at peace.

"Where did you find it?" he says again, tying the two frayed ends of twine together.

Do I tell him? I shouldn't lie to him. Lying is wrong and would be the quickest path to my punishment. Plus, I must tell him for the sake of Sister Brigitte.

That's what I do. I tell him the full account, my nervous fingers plucking at my belt. It doesn't take long for his joy to melt into sorrow and finally into a blank stare that I've never seen on the face of a monk before. 'Tis almost as if his soul has been wrapped in a dark shadow.

"You are the *L* on the cave wall, aren't you?" I ask him when I've finished. He doesn't owe me any answer. I'm just a girl, and he's an obedientiary monk that the abbot put in charge of Penwood Manor.

He presses his back against the wall and sinks to the stairs, the tips of his leather shoes sticking out from the bottom of his robe. He hasn't stopped clinging to the clover this entire time, even after his face turned white hearing Sister Brigitte's name, realizing this day might be her very last one on earth.

We don't speak for a long while—I gazing out the entrance at the boys running past, and he clasping the parchment and the clover in silence. The joy on his face has been suffocated and replaced with pain and regret. *And guilt?* Maybe my suspicions are true, then.

"You know that I must tell Mother Abbess about this," I say to him finally. "I'm sorry, Brother." It would be wrong for me to keep secrets from the abbess about such things. Still, I feel sympathy for poor Brother Leo. I've never seen him this way—not angry or gruff or joyful, just blank and empty and wounded.

He stops staring at the stone and turns to me with a tear in his eye, squeezing the clover 'twixt both his thumbs. "Do not be too hasty in your judgment, Lucy," he says, in a tone I haven't heard from him before. "You must first hear my full account of what happened 'twixt us."

"That's not necessary," I say. I'm just a girl. Why does he feel obligated to answer to me as though he is reporting to his abbot? I cannot judge him or forgive his sins. I am no priest.

He folds his arms. "I will not have you spreading scandal," he says. "*Please*, Lucy. Listen."

I give a nod and lean my back against the edge of the door. He sits across from me on the stairs, forlorn. I must trust that God chose me out of all the girls at the convent to speak with Sister Brigitte this morning. That must be the reason I'm here, though 'tis still a mystery to me.

"I grew up with Brigitte when I was just a lad at Tatecastre Manor," he says, his eyes reliving a season long past. "Our two families spent Sunday afternoons in the meadow together, picking clovers and feasting on fruit and bread. The fullness of Brigitte's hair . . . the deep wells of her eyes—she was a girl whose beauty could capture the heart of any knight or prince."

He pauses, and a smile returns to his cheeks. Except Sister Brigitte is now the bride of Jesus; Brother Leo must realize that. When he sees the expression on my face, he grows red and the smile dies on his lips.

"For a time, I fancied to make her my wife." His eyes fall back into sorrow. "Her father refused to agree to it—I was not her equal, you see. He forbade our union and confronted my family, threatening to make trouble for us in the village."

I know how headstrong fathers can be. I asked Father many times to let me stay at home during his journeys with our manor lord. With no living mother to care for me, he refused to hear of it. That's how I wound up at Harwood Abbey. Yet hasn't my life changed for the better being here this past year?

Brother Leo clutches the clover so tightly that his knuckles turn white. "After that, my family sent me to live with our cousins in York. Yet I hoped to return home one day and win Brigitte's hand." He sighs. "'Twas not to be. One evening in spring, word reached me in York that Brigitte's father had promised her in marriage to a nobleman's son. I realized then that my longing for her would never be fulfilled."

He puts his hands on his knees and falls into a silence I should not interrupt. How terrible it must have been for him to know that the girl he loved was betrothed to another.

"I despaired and wept and prayed for wisdom," he says finally. "After a month, I knew what I must do. My uncle was a black monk, as were three of my cousins. I realized that my heart was not intended for any living woman, but only for God alone. That is when I decided to come here as a novice."

"I understand," I say.

Brother Leo shrugs. "You may be surprised to hear that my soul felt at peace with my decision. Indeed, I took comfort in the solitude and prayers of my new life here. 'Twas a peace I had not thought possible." He seems lost in a memory from those days—the earliest years after Harwood Abbey's founding.

"Sister Brigitte never did marry that nobleman, did she?" I ask after a moment.

His chin bows low to his chest. "I remember well the day Brigitte arrived at Harwood Abbey. I had been here about a year, and one of my duties at that time was to manage the abbey's supplies. That afternoon, I walked the eastern trail past the convent to fetch our winter provisions from the old storage cave. Brigitte must have seen me from the convent garden."

I'm quite familiar with that garden. Sister Regina and I sometimes sit and talk with Xan there on Sunday afternoons. You can see the path from the garden wall, where the purple flowers grow.

"She caught up to me near the cave," he says, "her sweet voice calling my name as from a long-forgotten dream." He sighs again. "She pressed her hands into mine and told me all that had happened in her life that year. As you have already guessed, Lucy, with the assistance of her uncle she had spurned the man her father had chosen. But her father was a petty, spiteful sinner. In his wrath he shut Brigitte away in this nunnery to become a Benedictine nun. Little did he know that I too had been sent here."

I can only imagine how Sister Brigitte must have felt, being dragged to Harwood Abbey against her will. No matter how we girls feel, the world always expects us to submit and obey. At times it makes me want to shriek! Will Father do the same to me if he doesn't find a man wealthy enough for me to marry? Would he even consider a poorer boy of my own choosing?

"She had no desire to be a nun, of course," Brother Leo continues. "That much was plain when she confessed her true love for me. But she had come too late." His tone is almost chanting now. "I told her that I had taken my final vows as a monk. I told her of the peace I had found at this abbey, and of the mystery that God can work in our hearts in a life of silence and prayer."

In the silence of the convent's chapel, I too have noticed the peace that prayer can bring.

"Brigitte did not believe my words," he says. "She gazed into my eyes and begged me to take her away from this place—for us to run away together across the channel to Normandy and live our lives free from her cruel father." He peers out the door into the sky. Does he wish he could fly away to that place in his dreams where they escape this abbey and defy all of Heaven and earth?

"What did you do?" I ask.

He shakes his head. "I jerked my hands from hers and turned away. I told her that seeking me out to speak together alone was a violation of the abbey's rules. That I must report the details of our meeting to my abbot. That I could never speak to her again. Indeed, that I must leave her that very instant."

It seems monks must obey too—just like girls—even if it hurts. "You did rightly, Brother."

"Nay." He shudders and bows his head in shame. "For at that very instant that she held my eyes, my faithless heart was tempted to agree to her plan, I must confess—to betray my vow to God and cast my soul's redemption to the grave. And in that moment she saw my struggle and hesitation."

What was she thinking, I wonder? Did Sister Brigitte believe he would yield to her request?

"She pleaded again for me to flee with her, before my abbot could prevent it." He breathes out sharply. "She told me that my eyes had betrayed me, and that she could never accept the life that her father was trying to force upon her. That she would never be happy at this abbey."

The disobedient girl Brother Leo described isn't the Sister Brigitte I have come to know—so submissive and humble in her ways. Something truly remarkable must have changed Sister Brigitte's heart to make her become such a saintly nun. "What happened?" I ask.

He holds up the shamrock stone, and it swings from the twine held tightly 'twixt his fingers. "I gave her this holy stone, hoping Saint Patrick would lead her to Jesus. I begged her to open her heart to the will of God. That our Lord works in mysterious ways. That she could still find peace in this life."

He stops speaking, and his story falters as he tries to rein in his emotions, I think.

"She didn't respond well," I guess aloud.

"Aye." He pulls himself to his feet, grasping the stair railing. "My moment of hesitation had ruined it all. My doubting eyes had confirmed her worst fears for her future. She burst out in anger, took the shamrock stone, and threw it as far into the woodland as her strength would allow." His eyes grow sorrowful at the memory. "Her final bitter words were to call me a coward who would rather pray than to find true love. Then she fled from me in tears."

There's no lie in Brother Leo's face, only humility and brokenness. "I never spoke with her again, but my heart grew more sorrowful as time passed. I imagined poor Brigitte resisting her vocation just to spite me and her father—rejecting the peace that comes from being one of Christ's little lambs."

Now I think I know why Brother Leo always has such ire in his voice. He is angry with himself. "You did your duty," I say—the same words I tell myself so often when I submit to this world's decrees.

He peers beyond me into the cloudy sky. "From that very day I began a deep and abiding penance, which I offered to God for the sake of Brigitte's soul and the purity of her vocation. I feared that her future years of solitude would be sorrowful ones due to my faults. The abbot allowed me to continue those penances even after Sister Brigitte took her final vows and became a nun."

Maybe that's why Brother Leo is always lecturing everyone about penance and suffering. Now 'tis clear why God sent me here today. Saint Patrick himself may be guiding my very steps and words.

"Brother," I say. "You must know that Sister Brigitte is widely held within our convent to be the happiest and most loving spouse of Christ—filled with devotion and brimming with joy at all times. She's an inspiration to me and every girl there, and I can see how much she's influenced the other nuns too."

His head raises as though it has suddenly become lighter.

"Your prayers are answered, Brother. Your penance was fruitful. I don't know what happened in the years since you knew Sister Brigitte, but she is no longer the disobedient girl that you described. She fell in love with her life here at the convent and took her final vows with a full heart. She is the most loved of Christ's little lambs, I assure you."

My words seem medicine for his ailing heart. Though he doesn't meet my eyes, I can sense the pain seeping from his heart and his years of self-anger draining from him. "This is true? She became all of that?"

"Aye, Brother—all of that and much more. She has been that way her whole life, as far as anyone at the convent knows. 'Til now I could never have guessed at what you've described to me."

More tears fill his eyes, but not the sad kind. "I have thought these many years that my shamrock was lost in the woodland—picked up by a stranger or dragged through the brush by an animal. Only now do I surmise what happened. Sister Brigitte must have recovered the clover from the forest that very day and kept it close to her. That holy shamrock must have worked a miracle within her heart, allowing her to make peace with the path of her life. Eventually, she must have deposited it in the cave where we parted."

"What about the *B* and *L* and *amor*?" I ask. "Why would she write that on the wall, since *amor* is a word used to describe the love of a man and woman?"

He ponders a moment. "That word has fuller meanings, Lucy. It can also describe our deep yearning for God. Perhaps Sister Brigitte wrote that word because the love we shared for each other had become bound up in the love we share for Christ our Lord."

I smile. "Then maybe your shamrock really does work miracles, Brother."

He caresses the clover again. "And 'tis returned to me on the day of Saint Patrick."

As surely as my heart beats, I know what must be done now.

"Come with me, Brother. See her one last time before she goes to be with Jesus. Reconcile any ill will 'twixt the two of you. Satisfy yourself that God has accepted your penance and answered your prayers."

Doubt crosses his brow. He looks to me for guidance, and I nod and smile. "Come, Brother."

He hesitates only a moment longer. "Aye," he says. "The abbot would approve. Let us go quickly!"

I stand outside the cell with Sister Regina and Sister Cecilia. They were surprised to see me arrive at the convent with Brother Leo by my side. As far as they know, he has never even spoken with Sister Brigitte. Still, the power of the moment presents no obstacle to God's will that Brother Leo should see Sister Brigitte one final time.

We watch from the open door as he enters Sister Brigitte's cell and stands next to her bed.

"Sister," he says softly. "'Tis I—Brother Leo."

Sister Regina warned us on the way to the cell that Sister Brigitte hasn't awakened all day. Yet, at the sound of Brother Leo's voice, her eyes spring open and a sweet smile brightens her face.

"Leo," she says. "You are . . . here."

He takes the clover pendant and places it upon her open palm.

"Come, Lucy," Sister Regina says, taking my hand. "You too, Cecilia."

We step away from the door and step down the hallway. "What is going on here, Lucy?" Sister Cecilia asks in a stern tone. No doubt she expects me to be as obedient as a novice, though I have taken no vows. Indeed, this must be the moment I'm supposed tell them what happened.

Why does my heart hesitate? Is this truly the kind of news that I must report?

God took a sad situation and turned it to good, as He always does. Not only did Brother Leo do penance from his abbot, but his prayers were answered a hundredfold.

"Well?" Sister Cecilia says.

"They are old friends," I say—and that is the truth, for did not Jesus say that no greater love could one person have for another than to lay down one's life for a friend? For the last forty years, Brother Leo has laid down his own life for the sake of Sister Brigitte's soul. That is the measure of true friendship.

Sister Cecilia seems unsatisfied, but we follow her back to the cell and Brother Leo.

Sister Brigitte is pushing the clover along the mattress toward Brother Leo's hand. "Thank you," she says to him. "If you had not . . . prayed for me . . . , I might never have become . . . Christ's true love."

Those are her very last words, I think.

Brother Leo takes the green clover into his hand and bends to kiss her forehead. "'Tis all part of the mystery of this life, dear sister." When he leaves the room, he seems filled with serenity.

We haven't even reached the front door when one of the other nuns cries out in grief. "Come quickly, sisters! Our sweet Brigitte has passed on from this life."

I'm not surprised. That healing reunion with Brother Leo was all that she'd been waiting for, wasn't it? The clover that she'd hidden in that cave those many years ago had been her final attachment to this world. By returning it to Brother Leo for her, I helped to bring them healing and peace, just as she'd told me.

Brother Leo turns to me and smiles. "Do not mourn today, Lucy. Rejoice for Sister Brigitte. Soon she will be walking with her true Love in Paradise."

Sister Regina looks at me curiously after Brother Leo departs, but she asks me only a single question. "Where did that shamrock stone come from?"

"'Twas a gift," I say. "A gift from Saint Patrick."

###

If you enjoyed this story, be sure to check out The Harwood Mysteries by Loyola Press. Lucy is a main character in that series, where she and her best friend, Xan, solve spooky mysteries at Harwood Abbey and beyond. Book One of the series, *Shadow in the Dark*, was released in July 2020, and Book Two, *The Haunted Cathedral*, was released in February 2021. The short story in this anthology takes place shortly after the events in Book One.

ABOUT THE AUTHOR

ANTONY B. KOLENC is the author of The Harwood Mysteries, an exciting historical-fiction series for youth published by Loyola Press. He is a long-time member of the Catholic Writers Guild, and his novels all have the Catholic Writers Guild Seal of Approval. He retired as a Lieutenant Colonel from the U.S. Air Force Judge Advocate General's Corps after 21 years of military service. A law professor who's had his works published in numerous journals and magazines, Kolenc now speaks at legal, writing, and home-education events. He and his wife, Alisa, are the parents of five children and have been blessed with three wonderful grandchildren. To learn more about The Harwood Mysteries and its author, visit www.AntonyKolenc.com.

1540, Renaissance England

LUCKY AND BLESSED

by Amanda Lauer

Honora dropped to her knees in the shadow of Fountains Abbey, a blanket of clover—or shamrocks, as they were called in her mother's homeland—cushioning her fall. Her mam, Margaret Thompson, had talked of the beauty of Ireland so often that Honora could picture every cliff and bog in her mind, even if she had never set foot on the Emerald Island herself. As a matter of fact, she'd never been more than a day's ride away from the Yorkshire estate upon which she'd been born.

When her mother was a child, she expected she'd live out her life out in Bray, County Wicklow, but a chance encounter on her way into Raheen-a-Cluig when she was sixteen, just shy of Honora's age now, changed the course of her life. Lester Thompson, First Baron of Markington, accompanying The Earl of Surrey, Thomas Howard—who had been sent from England to Ireland in 1520 to regain control of the island for King Henry VIII—happened to catch a glimpse of the blue-eyed, raven-haired lass as she stepped into the stone church.

In the words of Honora's parents, Cupid's arrow hit its mark. Regardless that England sought to subjugate the Irish and that the young man and young woman should have been sworn enemies, love won the day. With their Catholic faith as common ground, the couple married soon after—in that very same church where Lester had first spied Margaret—and then settled at the Thompson estate in Yorkshire, along the western coast of Great Britain.

Honora let out a sigh as she surveyed the groundcover beneath her. She ran her fingers over the feather-soft foliage, searching as she always did for the elusive four-leaf clover. Despite weeks of diligently hunting—and praying to Saint Anthony—she had yet to find one.

Seeing as none of the prayers she had offered up for the primary concerns in her life had been answered, she held out hope that this tiny request would be fulfilled. She was desperate for the luck that a four-leaf clover was said to bestow on the person fortunate enough to find one.

Suddenly, the hairs on Honora's arms stood on end. She felt someone's eyes on her. Trying to maintain a casual air, she surveyed the area around her. From her spot on the ground, all she could see was the abandoned shell of the abbey.

Remaining perfectly still, she listened for a few moments as a doe would when sensing danger nearby. Hearing nothing, she relaxed a bit. Perhaps the tales she'd heard were actually true and some of the monks escaping during the Dissolution of the Monasteries had indeed turned into fairy folk.

"Is it thee, fairy folk?" she whispered. "Have you come back to visit your monastery?" Honora turned her ear toward the abandoned building, listening for a response.

And a response was precisely what she got. Laughter. But not the trill of a fairy giggle as she'd expected. More of a muffled guffaw, as a human voice would produce. Make that a human *male* voice. Immediately, Honora gathered her items, jumped to her feet, and backed away from the stone structure.

Ambrose clenched his teeth together. He hadn't meant to be heard. But the sweet voice from that enchanting young lady had caught him by surprise. Judging from what she'd said, it was obvious that she hadn't spent the last four years of *her* life with monks. Otherwise, she'd have known beyond a shadow of a doubt that those men had neither the inclination nor—for a number of them— the build to transform into fairies. A stout fairy would never be able to clear the ground.

He'd noticed the girl as she'd approached the monastery minutes before. Crouching behind the tumbled wall, he observed her to see what she was about. Ambrose had been tucked in this spot for the last day, and she was the first human that he'd seen. And a fine specimen of a human she was. After living exclusively with monks since the age of fourteen, she was a sight for sore eyes.

"I heard you. Show thyself," commanded the lass in what Ambrose imagined was meant to be an authoritative voice. The shakiness of her tone gave her away though.

With his position breeched, he considered finding an escape route through the back of the ramshackle structure, but something urged him to face his adversary, if that's what she proved to be.

Ambrose peeked over the half-tumbled wall, and seeing no one accompanying the girl, stood to his full height. He guessed the girl to be around his age, maybe slightly younger.

"State your name and your business on this property," the girl stuttered out, pointing a wooden spoon at him menacingly.

Biting his lower lip to keep the smile from his face, he dutifully replied, "Ambrose, m'lady."

"Mister Ambrose . . ."

"Technically, it's Master Ambrose. I shan't be eighteen until next month."

"Noted, Master Ambrose," she replied with a bit less of an edge to her voice. "This land is private property. Why are you here?"

"Seeing that this land belongs to the Church, or did," Ambrose noted, surveying the missing interior walls, "I could be asking you the same question."

"Don't try weaseling your way out of answering," the girl shot back. "I'm the one making the inquiries, not you. Come out with it now, or I'll be notifying the authorities."

Authorities? Highly unlikely, but in the interest of keeping the conversation going, Ambrose acquiesced and gave her an abbreviated explanation.

"Under His Majesty's orders, Byland Abbey has been

dissolved. In the chaos of his troops ascending on the building to begin dismantling it, the brethren scattered," he said. "I was hoping that King Henry—not wishing to further distance himself from His Holiness—would spare Fountains Abbey, as it's the largest Cistercian community in Yorkshire. So, I took my chances and made my way here."

The girl's sapphire blue eyes widened. *Perhaps she had not heard the fate of Byland Abbey?*

Her consternation was revealed a moment later.

"You're a monk?"

The wooden spoon fell from Honora's hand, ricocheting off a rock and landing near the monastery wall. *This was not good. Being disrespectful to a member of the clergy was a sin. Maybe not mortal, but most certainly venial. Only God knows when I'll be able to find a confessor and erase this stain from my soul.*

King Henry VIII had orchestrated the Dissolution of the Monasteries four years ago. It was not supported by the majority of his subjects, including Honora's father. Those holy institutions were the bedrock of English life. Monasteries provided education and charity for their surrounding neighbors, were used as medical facilities, and offered lodging for passing travelers as well.

Earlier this year, the abbot and thirty monks residing at Fountains Abbey had been pensioned off and removed from the grounds. The crown promptly melted down the valuable lead from its roofs and pipes to finance the king's never-ending wars.

The building was sold to their neighbor, Sir Reginald Grisham—a merchant and member of parliament—who further despoiled the sacred site by stripping the stone, timber, and remaining lead from the structure to help defray the cost of his purchase.

"No," replied the young man before her.

The blunt reply snapped Honora back to attention.

"No, what?"

"No, I'm not."

"Not a monk?"

Ambrose shook his head. That explained why his dome was left unshaven. Honora couldn't help but admire the loose curls of his short locks. His dark brown hair was the perfect complement to his azure-colored eyes—the hue of the sky on a clear summer day—and her favorite color at that.

A slight smile came to Honora's lips. Not a moment later, another startling thought came to her.

"You're studying to be a monk, then?" She locked eyes with Ambrose, lifting her brows as she awaited his answer.

"I am a second son," he replied evenly.

So much for this man being an answer to her prayers. Honora's hopes were quashed by his declaration. He had his own obligations to fulfill.

Heaving a sigh, she sank back to her knees.

The lass took the news of his "calling" just about as poorly as Ambrose had when his father had laid out plans for his life five years ago. The Earl of Ormond, George Butler, and his wife, Lady Mairead Fitzgerald, had been profoundly blessed to produce seven male progeny. Their oldest son would inherit the title and the family estate upon the earl's passing. Following custom, the second son was to be sent to the Church and the third son to the military.

As a child, Ambrose received a well-rounded education, mirroring the disciplines in which King Henry had been tutored in his youth, including Latin, grammar, theology, history, rhetoric, philosophy, arithmetic, logic, literature, geometry, and music.

When he outpaced his tutor, Ambrose's father had turned his education over to the monks at Byland Abbey. He embraced the faith, yet he felt no pull toward the religious life. Truth be told, Ambrose had little interest in running an estate either. He had a passion for designing and building. If it were up to him, he'd make his living creating grand structures such as churches, glorifying God with the talents that He had bestowed upon him.

Having harbored doubts about a religious calling before, his misgivings had been magnified tenfold over the span of the last few minutes. Something about the girl before him tugged at his heartstrings.

Curiosity getting the better of him, he put forth a question. "May I have your name, m'lady?"

The girl tilted her chin up to meet his gaze, a forlorn expression in her eyes. "Honora, sir. Honora Thompson . . . Daughter of the First Baron of Markington,

Lester Thompson."

It was Ambrose's turn to be surprised. The baron was a legend amongst the professed religious. When the Dissolution of the Monasteries began, Thompson broke the law by providing safe shelter to a number of monks who'd been turned out of the monasteries.

Someone had reported him to the local constable, and Thompson was arrested and imprisoned on the count of high treason. Convicted of his crime, he was executed on Tower Hill three years ago, June 30, in the year of the Lord 1537.

"I'm so sorry for your loss."

"God rest his soul." Honora made the Sign of the Cross, and he followed suit.

Although Ambrose was wont to be more deliberate before acting, he detached the sword from his belt and set it on the partially dismantled wall. With his left hand on the stones for support, he cleared the barrier between him and the girl and landed next to her on the patch of clover.

It pained him to see such beautiful eyes dulled by sadness. Instinctively, he knelt down before Honora and grasped her hands between his.

Caught completely unaware, Honora stiffened when Ambrose's hands went around hers. The only male who had ever been in such close proximity to her before had been her father. And, although she was sure that he cared about her as any father would his own offspring, he'd never been one for displaying affection toward his child.

It didn't take long, however, for the warmth of Ambrose's grip to melt the protective armor that she'd worn around her heart for three long years.

He said nothing as he held her hands, but Honora could feel the sheer strength emanating from his body. Second son or not, he seemed better suited to a life of hard work and adventure than one of prayer and meditation.

Although they had just met, she sensed that Ambrose was concerned about her well-being. At least that made one person in this lonely world who cared. Even her mother had forgotten her.

Completely unbidden, a tear slipped from her eye. She sniffled, trying to hold in her emotions.

Relinquishing his hold on her, Ambrose used his free hand to tilt Honora's chin up so he could look into her eyes.

"I didn't mean to upset you by bringing up such a sad topic," he said sincerely.

"Think naught of it," said Honora. "It's good to say my father's name out loud again. No one speaks of him to me anymore. Actually, few people have spoken to me at all since the incident."

The look in Ambrose's eyes told Honora that he found her proclamation hard to believe.

"Like the good monks, my mother and I were cast from our manor after my father's death. Thankfully we were allowed to set up house in the gardener's cottage. All but one servant left us. Beatrice had been by my mother's side since she was her nursemaid and has remained loyal to her to this day."

Leaning back on his haunches, Ambrose clasped her hands between his once again.

A tingling sensation flowed through Honora. She cast her eyes down so the young man wouldn't see the flush coming to her cheeks.

"They say that sharing your grief with another person can help ease the pain of loss," noted Ambrose. "Would you like to tell me about your father?"

Honora considered his offer. *Could he be trusted?* Raising her head, she searched the depths of Ambrose's eyes. The blue was so clear that she swore she could see into his soul. Deciding to follow her intuition, she began.

"When the first monastery in Yorkshire was gutted, a group of monks arrived on our doorstep soon after. It was the middle of the night and my parents invited them into the manor house. After discussing it privately, the two announced that the Lord had shown them that the Thompson family must help those displaced men."

It was only to be once, Honora recalled. "The plan was to hide the monks until passage could be secured for them to cross the English Channel into France. Wales would have been an easier escape route, but with the passage of the Acts of Union in 1536, English law had been extended into Wales."

Honora thought back to another key event that same year. "Despite being morally opposed to many of the king's decrees, my father had stayed out of the fray for our family's safety. But, after the Pilgrimage of Grace uprising was suppressed and the leaders were executed, he could no longer stand by. Our house became a safe haven for both men and women religious."

Biting her lip to stem the flow of tears, she continued. "We did everything to keep our operation under cover, but we were warned that someone had betrayed us. The refugees staying with us were sent on their way immediately. My father bravely stood his ground and met the king's soldiers as they came onto our property. That was the last time I saw him alive."

Ambrose squeezed Honora's hands to comfort her. While it was sinful to disparage another human being, he couldn't help but question King Henry VIII's motives and some of the decisions that he'd made concerning his subjects over the last decade or so.

It could actually be traced back to 1517 with the publication by Martin Luther—himself a monk and a theologian at that time—of "The Ninety-Five Theses," calling into question some of the basic tenets of Roman Catholicism. Eventually that led him and his followers to sever ties with the Church and begin the Protestant Movement.

Even though King Henry had continued to practice the Catholic faith, it seemed that he found this divide the ideal time to seek an annulment of his marriage to Catherine of Aragon, who'd had no male issue that had lived past infancy. Word had spread even as far as Yorkshire that for years he'd had his eyes set on making Anne Boleyn his wife. Thus, he was determined to do everything in his power to get a dispensation from Pope Clement VII to dissolve his first marriage.

With the thought to take Honora's mind off her father, Ambrose changed the course of their conversation slightly to share something that she could find interesting.

"If things had turned out differently, Anne Boleyn may very well have been my mother."

She peered at him quizzically. "How's that?"

"When my father was a young man, he joined the household of Cardinal Wolsey, who was King Henry's almoner. The man was in charge of distributing money to the deserving poor throughout the kingdom. Believe it or not, the king suggested that my father marry his cousin Anne Boleyn to resolve a dispute between their two families."

Honora pulled back, straightened up, and gave Ambrose her complete attention.

"For some reason," he continued, "the negotiations came to a standstill. My father then went on to marry my mother, Lady Mairead Fitzgerald."

"Fitzgerald," said Honora in surprise. "As in *the* Fitzgeralds?"

Ambrose nodded in affirmation.

"You're related to King Henry's cousin Silken Thomas Fitzgerald, the Lord Chancellor of Ireland?" Honora hastily crossed herself. "God bless his immortal soul."

Honora's heart fluttered with compassion. Or some

other feeling. It was difficult to determine.

Thomas Fitzgerald—known as the unofficial King of Ireland—had been executed after a failed rebellion against the crown three years ago.

The revelation about Anne Boleyn caused a shiver to go down Honora's spine.

If Ambrose's father had married that woman, maybe Henry never would have attempted to divorce the saintly Catherine of Aragon.

When the pope refused to annul the marriage, King Henry split from the Catholic Church and bestowed Royal Supremacy upon himself, along with the title of Supreme Head of the Church of England.

Thinking of the king caused Honora to grind her teeth. Her life had fallen apart because of that arrogant man and his lust for power.

"I'll have you know that I met King Henry once," Honora said after some consideration.

"Did you, now? Where?" asked Ambrose curiously.

"Not far from this very spot, on our ancestral lands. Or, I should say, the lands that were once ours." Honora took a breath and continued.

"It was ten years ago. The king and Her Royal Highness were touring the crown's provinces. They stopped with their entourage at our manor to pay their respects to my father. I'll admit, at the age of seven, I was quite taken with the man. On his steed he held himself with such aplomb, he seemed as though he were a god to my younger self."

Ambrose's eyebrows shot up.

"After he dismounted, I'd stared at him tongue-tied. With his devilishly handsome good looks, trim physique and confident swagger, what young girl wouldn't be rendered speechless?"

Noting that Ambrose couldn't hide his indignation, Honora quickly added, "Of course, he wouldn't hold a candle to such a fine man as yourself."

"Of course," said Ambrose, going along with her assertion.

Actually, had he been able to read Honora's mind, the young man before her would have realized that her words weren't in jest. Whilst her experience around males had been limited to the older villagers and workers on their family's land, she knew an attractive and honorable man when she saw one.

Returning to her story, Honora continued, "When I was finally able to regain my wits, I curtseyed before the king, as any loyal subject would do. The man bestowed on me his rakish smile and gave me a convivial wink. I remember it as though it were yesterday."

Ambrose rolled his eyes.

"Just to set the record straight, Master Ambrose, I never considered the encounter to be anything more than happenchance . . ."

"That seems logical."

"Until two weeks ago."

Ambrose felt his hackles rise. Jaw clenched, he nodded to Honora to encourage her to proceed with her story.

"Our neighbor, Sir Reginald Grisham, who now owns this monastery and the grounds on which it stands, paid a visit to me and my mother at the gardener's cottage a fortnight ago."

The expression on his face must have signaled his ire, because Honora quickly added, "Don't misunderstand me. I am indebted to the king for choosing to spare our lives and allowing us to have a roof over our heads, as humble as it may be. And, I believe my mother would concur. That is, if she could speak. She's uttered nary a word since she witnessed my father's beheading."

Furrowing his eyebrows, Ambrose pressed for more information. "I see. Who now lives in the manor?" Intrigue in the girl increased with each passing minute.

"The aforementioned Sir Reginald. He is the financier who acts on behalf of the king."

"Is he?"

"I've known the man my entire life. To be honest, I'd always felt a bit uneasy around him. But I must say, since my father's passing, he's been nothing short of solicitous."

"I'm sure he has." *She may be reassured, but I'm not sure that I can say the same thing.*

"I do my best to be charitable and see God in every person I meet," said Honora. "Sir Reginald knows the dire circumstances that I'm facing. He claims to be looking out for my best interests."

"Dire circumstances?"

Honora appeared to be uncomfortable but answered nonetheless. "We've been left nearly penniless. There is no dowry money," she said, biting her lip.

"You were to be married, then?"

"One way or another. Parties were negotiating before King Henry broke with the Church. My father was striving to find a suitor who would enhance our family's social status. If that fell through, I was to become a bride of Christ."

Dowry or not, no religious vows would be spoken for the foreseeable future by anyone. In addition to the monasteries, priories, and friaries, even convents were now being disbanded. There were close to a thousand religious houses in England before this rampage started, but who knew how many would be left when it finally ended?

Doing her best to display a cheerful demeanor and to show Ambrose that her faith in God remained unshaken, Honora went on. "Since my father's passing, I've endeavored to forgive the people who brought about his execution. And, I strive to find some good in each day. Hard as it is at times . . ."

"That is noble of you," he said sincerely. "I'm not sure that I could do the same."

Warmth crept to Honora's cheeks. The compliment caught her off guard. She was momentarily left without words.

Ambrose broke the silence. "What brings you here on this beautiful day, fair lady?"

Now the warmth extended to the tips of her ears. Such a

smooth talker. Perhaps he'd make a good monk after all. His sermons could prove quite inspiring.

Blinking hard to regain her composure, Honora recalled the question and endeavored to give him an answer that wouldn't sound childish. *Of course, he's heard me call out to the fairies, so that may be pointless.*

"I find comfort sitting in the shadow of this monastery. The monks who lived and worked here were not only our neighbors but our friends as well."

He seemed satisfied with that answer, but there was more to it than that. "And . . . I was here searching for something."

Eyeing her closely, Ambrose prompted her to proceed. "And that was . . . ?"

Honora dropped her hands to her lap. "I was in search of a clover."

He cocked his head toward her. "A clover? You're surrounded by such foliage. That couldn't have proven to be that difficult of a task."

"Not just any clover, Master Ambrose. A four-leaf clover."

His eyebrows raised in curiosity. "So, you believe the old-wives' tale of four-leaf clovers bringing luck to their finders?"

Honora hesitated. Generally, she wasn't of a superstitious nature but she was at the end of her rope. "I don't know that I do," she admitted after some thought. "But my prayers have been ignored thus far and I'm running out of time and options."

"Let me get this straight, m'lady." Ambrose imagined how she'd come to be there. "You've trekked to the middle of this forest, armed with just a wooden spoon for protection, in search of an elusive mystical clover?"

"To be certain, the spoon wasn't my means of defending myself," said Honora matter-of-factly. "It was to dig out the clover by the roots if I found one."

Ambrose viewed her amusedly.

"Trust me, kind sir, if I were to find this clover, I'd want to keep the entire plant so I may keep luck in continual supply," she retorted with a twinkle in her eyes. "We've been sorely lacking in that lately."

"Have you?" The encounter with this sweet lass had been unexpected, but welcome. Ambrose enjoyed the lilt of Honora's voice. But, even more so, he enjoyed perusing the vision of loveliness before him. The royal blue dress she wore had seen better days, but the style with the high waist, square neckline bordered with gold brocade, and the long trailing sleeves, enhanced her trim figure.

In a resigned tone, Honora continued. "As I mentioned before, I've no dowry. Even if I had, the prospects for marriage grow dimmer by the day. Most girls are married by my age. I'd resigned myself to spend the rest of my life caring for my mother, but her time on earth is coming to an end, I fear."

Ambrose felt compassion for this girl but had to hold in a laugh when she spoke of herself as though she were too ancient to be eligible to wed. Between her charming character, lovely features, enchanting eyes, and the intricately braided hair that fell to her waist, he could imagine no more appealing bride. From his perspective, God had been saving Honora for the perfect mate. *Could it perhaps be me?*

His eyes widened as he pondered that thought. Politely, he responded to her previous comment. "So sorry to hear about your mother, Honora."

She gave him a slight smile. "For three years I'd hoped she'd awaken from her grief, but it's gradually sapping the life from her. She spends her days rocking in a chair set before the fireplace, her eyes entranced by the flames. Her maidservant Beatrice and I do what we can to engage her, but she's lost the will to live. I feel that she will be reunited with my father in heaven soon."

"What will happen with you when she passes?"

"I've given that question a good deal of thought lately. As I have no claim to the cottage in which we live, in most likelihood, I'll be evicted. I've considered hiring myself out as a washerwoman in the village, but opportunities such as that are scarce now with all the women religious searching for work themselves."

The thought of Honora spoiling her alabaster hands performing manual labor distressed him. Regardless of the fact that he may be disowned by his father for not fulfilling the religious duties of a second son, Ambrose felt his heart drawn to this girl. With conviction, he cleared his throat to offer her his assistance.

Before he could get a word out, Honora made a pronouncement that stopped him dead in his tracks.

"It seems as though fate has intervened in my life. When Sir Reginald came to our doorstep the week before last, he had correspondence from His Royal Majesty. I'm to leave tomorrow at sunrise for London—accompanied by Sir Reginald—to take residence in Hampton Court Palace. I've been offered a position as lady-in-waiting for King Henry VIII's new wife, Catherine Howard."

While Honora assumed Ambrose to be adept at hiding his feelings, her announcement must have come as a bit of a shock to him. After clamping his jaw shut, he peppered her with questions.

"The king chose you himself?"

"From what the note said, it appears that he did," said Honora.

"Why on earth would he call for someone from Yorkshire? Well-educated and refined young women litter the streets of London."

Honora felt herself blush. She didn't want to sound conceited so she weighed her words carefully before speaking. "He said he had been quite 'taken' with me when we met. Apparently, he'd been waiting for the ideal time to invite me to be part of his household."

Ambrose pursed his lips. Honora could see why that would make a person wonder. Ten years was a long time.

She hastily continued. "I was just a child when we met. With everything that went on with my father, I believe the king wanted to give me time to put that behind me so I'd be in a better state of mind to accept his request."

With the skeptical mien still on Ambrose's face, Honora plowed ahead. "Seeing that Catherine and I are the same age; it sounds as though Henry feels that I'd be the ideal companion for her."

"This was all in the letter presented to you?"

"Essentially. Sir Reginald clarified the details for me."

"He did now, did he? Interesting that he is in such close counsel to the king."

Honora shrugged her shoulders. "What do I know of royal business?"

"Let me get this straight. You say that tomorrow Sir Reginald will be escorting you to London. That trip will take at least three days. Who will be your chaperone?"

"Why, Sir Reginald, of course." Honora did her best to sound assured, but she'd questioned the arrangement herself. "He's old enough to be my father. And we'll have a driver as well for protection."

Ambrose crossed his arms across his chest and locked eyes with her.

Was it possible that his misgivings were even stronger than her own?

King Henry wasn't the only one "taken" with this young lady, thought Ambrose. Instinctively, he felt the need to defend Honora. Somehow or other, over the course of one afternoon, she'd managed to pickpocket his heart right from his chest.

If something happened to her and he'd had a chance to prevent it and didn't, he'd never forgive himself.

Even if Sir Reginald was above reproach, the far greater concern may be what faced Honora when she arrived at court. A naïve and innocent thing such as herself would be eaten alive in that place.

"I barely know you, yet I'm not comfortable with that arrangement."

"I appreciate your concern, Master Ambrose, but everything is set. I've already told Sir Reginald that I would accept the offer from the king. His Majesty has been extremely gracious to allow me to serve him at court. I cannot go back on my word."

Had she not heard of the goings on at the palace? While the courtiers professed to being Christians, from what his father told him, it was a façade generally discarded behind closed doors.

King Henry dodged the arrow of having his soul barred from entering the gates of heaven by disavowing excommunication when he created the Church of England. His church also, to accommodate his whims, permitted divorce. Yet, he hadn't completely abandoned the Catholic faith and was allegedly a daily Communicant. But he was by no means the epitome of morality.

"Perhaps you should give it another week or two before you depart so you can think this through more thoroughly," suggested Ambrose.

"I've done nothing but think for the past fourteen days. Besides, it would be rude to ask Sir Reginald to reschedule the trip. I'm sure it's taxing enough on his schedule to escort me to London as it is."

"How about I be your escort? I'm sure I can scrounge up a means of transport."

Honora hesitated for a moment, biting her lower lip. "I couldn't ask you to do such a thing. There must be some monastery standing yet so you can resume your studies."

Whether there was or wasn't made no difference to him. If anything had been revealed to Ambrose over the course of the afternoon, it had been that the religious life was not his vocation. Where life would take him, who knew? He'd face that—and his father's ire—when the time came.

"I'm in no rush to return to my studies. I would very much like to help you."

"Your offer is nothing short of kind, but I can't accept it," said Honora with finality. "It would be improper to be escorted by a man your age. Whether you're to take religious vows or not."

Honora waited for Ambrose's response. If he insisted that she take him up on his offer, she would agree. Proper or not, she felt safe in his presence.

But no plea was issued in his behalf. Instead, he stood up, gently pulling her after him. Once firmly on her feet, he requested that she shut her eyes and hold out her right hand.

As perplexed as she was, she complied. A tingle went down her spine when Ambrose placed one hand under hers and then, using his other hand, gently set a small, cool object on her palm.

"Since you won't accept my offer to escort you to the

palace, I would beg of you to receive this gift."

Honora's heart beat loudly in her chest. She couldn't remember the last time someone had given her a present.

"May I open my eyes now?"

"Please do."

A gasp emitted from Honora's lips. Nestled in the middle of her hand was a piece of Connemara marble. She knew it distinctly because her mother had a chunk of it from her homeland. But this flat, circular stone, in varying shades of Irish green and a bit of brown swirled together, appeared to have been made by nature into the shape of a clover.

"It's not a four-leaf clover, but I'd like to think it will bring thee luck, nonetheless," said Ambrose, a smile lighting his face and revealing a sturdy set of well-placed teeth. They were as bright as hers, Honora noted.

Returning the broad smile, she wrapped her hand tightly around the clover. "Where did you ever find this? It's lovely."

"While searching for any Biblical transcripts that may have been discarded, I found this treasure. In their haste to vacate this building, the monks must have left it behind."

Honora sighed, overwhelmed for a moment by a stirring in her heart. "It feels . . . special . . . like a relic or something."

"Actually, that may be true." Ambrose gazed at the object in her hand. "A rolled parchment lay beside it, so I retrieved that as well. The archaic writing was not easy to decipher but I gather that the stone came directly from

Ireland and was used as an instrument to teach about the Blessed Trinity."

She sucked in a breath and looked up at him. "Wouldn't that be something if this had actually been Saint Patrick's?"

"That would be something."

Honora turned the stone over and inspected it closer, running her fingers along its edges. Giving a sigh, she stuck her hand out toward Ambrose, the shamrock nestled in her palm.

"Ambrose, I'm touched by your kindness and generosity, but I cannot accept this. You found it. You deserve to keep it." She stared into his eyes, getting lost in his sky-blue orbs. "You'll be in as much need of luck as I'll be."

"I insist," he replied, wrapping her fingers around the marble clover. "Besides, we know, as children of God, we are both lucky and blessed."

Smiling up at him, Honora nodded. "Yes, Divine Providence." She at once realized the folly of her search for a lucky clover, for truly God was over all and holding her in His grace.

"May I have the ribbon from your hair?" he asked. "A hole has been drilled through the top of the stone. We can string the ribbon through it and you can wear it around your neck."

Honora reached up and untied the ribbon that had been wound through her braids. Rolling the end of the fabric into a point, Ambrose poked the ribbon into the hole and pulled it through the stone.

"May I?" he asked, holding up the necklace.

"Of course." Honora turned her back to him. He reached his arms past her and then secured the ribbon around her neck. Once done, he gave her shoulders a squeeze, lingered behind her for a moment, and then stepped away to admire the ensemble.

Honora dropped her eyes to the pendant hanging above the neckline of her dress. She felt the warmth of Ambrose's hand as it brushed against her skin. He held the stone between his fingers.

"All I ask is that you make me two promises," he said softly.

Mechanically, Honora nodded her head, caught up in his gaze.

"First, I request that you remember me when you wear this."

Once again, Honora's head bobbed. "I shall."

Ambrose regarded her solemnly. "If things don't work out as you've planned, find me. You'll have my protection and assistance."

Before he knew what was happening, Honora threw her arms around his waist. Ambrose responded in kind, pulling her tightly to his chest. He inhaled deeply, reveling in the scent of fresh air and wildflowers in her hair.

If he had his druthers, he'd have held onto her forever, but glancing at the sky, he saw the sun sinking behind the walls of the monastery.

"Honora, my sweet, as much as I'd like to prolong our time together, I would imagine your maidservant will wonder where you are if you don't return to the cottage soon."

Ambrose felt her take in a deep breath and then slowly exhale.

"'Tis true," she replied, a catch in her voice.

"Will you allow me to walk you back?"

Honora disengaged from their embrace and nodded in agreement. Tears glistened on her lower eyelashes.

It was like a knife to the heart for Ambrose. Why had God led him to this very place, to meet this most wondrous creature, and then torn them apart just hours later? It was as though he'd been allowed a glimpse of heaven and then just as quickly, a veil dropped to shroud it from view. It didn't seem fair.

Pulling her shoulders back, Honora stepped away from the abbey towards a path that led into the forest. Awakening from his reverie, Ambrose caught up to her in three strides. He reached out and grabbed her hand.

Initially, he felt Honora tense up, but she relaxed as they set off hand in hand. Several minutes later she spoke.

"How shall I find you?"

"Leave word with Edward Butler. He'll know where to locate me."

Honora stopped dead in her tracks and dropped her hand from Ambrose's grip.

"The Earl of Ormond? How on earth would he know your whereabouts?"

Ambrose faced Honora and gave a blunt reply. "The Earl of Ormond is my father."

Silence hung between the two of them for the remainder of their journey. Honora was ashamed that she had been so brazenly casual with the Earl of Ormond's son. Her cheeks burned in mortification.

Relief swept over her when the cottage came into view. On the edge of their property, Honora stopped, gave Ambrose a respectful curtsy, and then made her goodbyes.

"Thank you for accompanying me, m'lord."

"Honora, this changes nothing between us," Ambrose insisted.

Giving him a sad smile, Honora turned away. She'd humiliated herself enough for one day. The last thing that she wanted was for him to see the tears streaming down her face. Without glancing back, she stepped across the threshold into the cottage and shut the wood plank door soundly behind her.

A restless night of sleep followed and before the rooster had a chance to crow, she was up and preparing for the trip. She shared a silent breakfast with her mother and Beatrice. Hearing a coach approaching, she bent down and gave her mother a hug, realizing that it could very well be the last time that they saw each other. Holding tight to the pendant around her neck, Honora choked back her tears, bade the maidservant farewell, grabbed her satchel, and walked out the door to greet Sir Reginald.

The man loaded her bag into the vehicle and then

helped her step into the enclosed space. They took seats across from each other. Once settled, the driver set off in the direction of London. The two shared pleasantries for a couple of minutes until the man broke off the conversation and sharply tapped the roof of the vehicle with his walking stick.

At once, the driver veered off the road into a field. Honora felt the hair rise on the back of her neck. Something wasn't right.

"Why have we left the main road?" she asked apprehensively.

"Nothing to fret about. We need to stop back at my estate," the man answered.

"Whatever for?"

"The trip is delayed."

Honora could feel the beat of her heart reverberate through her skull. This was a worrisome turn of events. If they weren't to travel immediately, then why had he bothered to fetch her today at all?

Sir Reginald continued. "Had your father not been so stubborn and insisted on negotiating for a suitor closer to your age, you'd have been my wife three years ago."

Honora shrank back into the far corner of the coach, horrified at the thought of this man as her husband. Her father had never mentioned such a thing to her.

"Alas, I was determined to have you . . . Sir Lester Thompson's blessing or not. How fortuitous that he was found to be a traitor to the monarchy and punished accordingly."

Stars floated in front of Honora's eyes. She blinked them back, willing herself not to swoon. "It was you who turned him in?" The thought horrified her. "We'd always seen you as a friend."

"Appearances can be deceiving," Sir Reginald replied with a sinister laugh. "Either way," he continued, "the odds were that your father would have been caught eventually. He thought with his heart rather than his head. Why he'd put his life on the line to save the skin of those tunic-wearing, rope-belted verse inscribers was beyond me."

I'm sure it was. Honora glared at the vile man.

"But, all's well that ends well, as they say," he noted. "You've no dowry so no man of good standing would take you as his wife. But, I'm willing to have you."

Honora blinked hard, not exactly sure what he meant by that statement.

Without warning, she saw something out of the corner of her eye as it flew past the carriage window. She suppressed a scream.

Glancing over his shoulder from his position on the carriage's driver's seat, Ambrose saw the previous occupant knocked out cold, lying along the side of the road. With him disposed of, it was now time to deal with the fiend inside the carriage with Honora.

Ambrose let the horse continue on for another minute and then brought the carriage to a halt. Not five seconds later, the vehicle shook as the roof was struck from the inside by what he assumed was a walking stick.

"Why have we stopped?" shouted Sir Reginald from the carriage interior.

Remaining silent, Ambrose crouched into position and waited for his prey to come into sight. Sure enough, the door slammed open, banging into the side of the wooden carriage, and out stepped the incensed man.

Before Reginald could pronounce one word, Ambrose sprang from the driver's seat and threw his whole weight into him. The force bowled the older man over, and his body slammed to the ground.

With the wind knocked out of his lungs and pinned to the dirt, Sir Reginald could barely choke out a threat. "Unhand me, you knave, or I'll have you beheaded."

"Just as you had Sir Lester Thompson?"

Hearing a gasp, Ambrose turned his head and noticed Honora at the door of the carriage, hand covering her gaping mouth.

With him momentarily distracted, Sir Reginald attempted to squirm from Ambrose's grasp, but he was no match for the younger and stronger man. Frustrated, he spat out, "That man was breaking the law, just as you are, you brigand."

"Seems to me that the pot may be calling the kettle black," Ambrose retorted. "From my position on the back of the carriage, I heard every word of your conversation with the young lady."

Honora stood in shock, watching the scene unfold

before her.

She was finally jolted back to reality when Ambrose asked her to grab the rope belt from his sack and assist him as he hog-tied her kidnapper.

Mission accomplished, Ambrose helped her back into the carriage and then unceremoniously rolled Sir Reginald to the side of the road.

"This is a warning, sir," ground out Ambrose. "You are never to lay a hand on this young lady again. Or the next time you will not only be tied up like a swine, you'll be put on a spit and roasted like one as well. Mark my words."

The man's face reddened. "You shan't get away with treating a member of the gentry so. You've stolen what was rightfully mine. I will hunt you down. You'll regret the day you first laid eyes on that girl."

Ambrose put his foot on the step that led to the open door of the carriage and looked deeply into Honora's eyes. Once again, her heart beat uncontrollably, but this time the sensation wasn't from fear, but something quite the opposite.

"I shall never regret the day we met, Honora," Ambrose said with conviction.

Sir Reginald prattled on, his voice muffled from his position on the ground. "I'll send King Henry's men after you. No one gets away with crossing His Majesty."

Eyes widened in concern, Honora looked at Ambrose. He stepped fully into the carriage and knelt at her feet. Putting one hand on each of her flushed cheeks, he gently placed a kiss on her forehead.

"I would protect you for life, if you'd have me." He leaned back and dropped his right hand to the Connemara clover pendant resting on her collar bone.

Honora didn't want to read more into his words than he intended. She replied guardedly. "I'm truly honored, Ambrose. Thank you." Honora clasped her hands around his fist so that the clover was in both of their grasps.

Waves of happiness, contentment, security and affection—or perhaps something more—washed over her.

"'Tis just as you said. You don't need to find a special clover to have good fortune. Our fortune is in God's hands."

Ambrose smiled brightly.

"That being said," Honora added pertly, "I'm still keeping the pendant. It may not be for good luck but every moment I'm wearing it, I'll remember how truly lucky and blessed I was to find you."

###

The Reformation, headed by former Augustinian monk Martin Luther, caused a time of inordinate upheaval throughout Europe. During the time of the Dissolution of the Monasteries, 1536 to 1541, King Henry VIII disbanded close to a thousand monasteries, priories, convents, and friaries in England, Wales and Ireland. This edict caused immense social problems and brought about great suffering to both the poor and the ordinary people living under his rule. If you enjoy Honora and

Ambrose's story set during these turbulent times and want to see how it plays out, a full-length novel about their adventures may be in the works down the road.

ABOUT THE AUTHOR

Devoted to her Catholic faith, AMANDA LAUER loves writing books—particularly Young Adult Historic Fiction—that portray the Church in a positive light and depict God's children endeavoring to become the best version of themselves every day. A journalist and proofreader by trade, Amanda embarked on her novelist career with the award-winning and best-selling Heaven Intended Civil War series. *A World Such as Heaven Intended* earned the 2016 YA CALA award. Currently, Amanda has several more books in the process of being published.

In addition to writing novels, Amanda works in the film industry writing and copy-editing screenplays. She was awarded Best Writer 2020 (Red Letter Awards) for her work as a co-writer on the movie *The Islands*.

When she's not at her computer writing, Amanda enjoys spending time with her family, which includes John, her husband of 40 years, children Stephanie, Nicholas, Samantha, and Elizabeth and their significant others, and seven of the most amazing and adorable grandchildren on this planet!

To learn more about Amanda, who's lucky and blessed to be living in a world such as heaven intended, visit her website: www.AmandaLauer.com.

19th Century, Johnstown, Pennsylvania, USA

5

DANKE

by Carolyn Astfalk

Cool water splashed William's bare forearms as the foot-long white fish wriggled from his line and plunged into the lake, its tailfin slapping the water as if waving goodbye. William growled and hurled the fishing rod to the ground where he stood on the reservoir bank, the remembered-taste of the oven-baked fish coated in melted butter slipping away as quickly as the fish itself.

Ma counted on him to bring home something to help feed his six siblings. For an Irish Catholic family, on Friday that meant fish, and lots of it. Maybe his older sister, Rose, now twenty years old, would bring home something from the South Fork Fishing and Hunting Club, where she worked in the clubhouse.

At fourteen, William had hoped to be hired by the elite western Pennsylvania club to help guests as they launched the fleet of fifty rowboats, canoes, little steamboats, and sailboats that dotted the four square miles of Conemaugh Lake during summer weekends, white sails waving over dark water that mirrored the tall pines, oaks, and chestnuts surrounding it. Only this summer hadn't turned out anything like previous summers. All the more reason for him to bring home something Ma could dish up for supper.

Determined, William plucked his pole from the ground and cast his line back into the lake. To the east, the sun continued its steady rise, peeking above the tree line and burning the mist that clung to the fringes of the lakeshore. He whistled a tune, one he remembered Pa singing late into the night when he and Ma had company and all but the oldest children, Rose and Dennis, were supposed to be in bed asleep.

His line jerked a couple of times, but he reeled in an empty hook both times, becoming more discouraged with each cast. Sunlight stretched across the water now, and on a rock mere yards away, a turtle sunned itself.

"Hey!" a familiar voice called from behind him. "What do you think you're doing?" William's seventeen-year-old brother, Dennis, strode toward him, his brows drawn together in irritation.

"Practicing my back stroke. What's it look like?" William turned back to the lake, broadening his stance, literally digging his heels in as he waited for the chiding he knew Dennis would give him.

Dennis, tall, fit, and handsome enough to attract attention from girls wherever he went, strode up alongside William, stopped, and planted his hands on his hips. "This is private property. You know you're not supposed to be fishing here." His gaze flicked to the opposite end of the lake, where cottages dotted the shore.

"Ah, they're not gonna miss a few fish." William reeled in the line, knowing despite his argument that Dennis would win and they'd be trekking home in time for a late breakfast. "What do they care if some poor kid pulls a bass out of their lake while they're back in the city?"

"Whether they care or not doesn't really matter, and you know it. And for the record, I think they do care. You know how they are." Dennis grimaced, probably still sore about how some of the snootier club guests had treated him while he'd been maintaining the grounds. Even in his menial position, he'd occasionally rubbed elbows with the club's millionaire members. Some were affable, some condescending, and others pretended he didn't exist.

"You know we need the food." William squared his shoulders and kept his eyes on his line, which drifted gently on the lake top as a breeze rustled the trees. "I'm old enough to contribute, to help Ma."

Dennis's weary sigh—probably weary because they'd had this conversation before—floated on the breeze. "I know. That's why I'm here."

William shot him a curious look but held fast to his rod.

"There's a small group coming today, despite the fever, and they'll be looking for fun on the lake. I asked if they could use someone to help deploy the boats, and—"

William's heart surged, and the rod dropped to the ground as he jumped and whooped, nearly tackling Dennis in the process. "You got me a job! Why didn't you say so in the first place?"

Dennis backpedaled, laughing. "Easy. It's only for the weekend. They're not hangin' around."

"Ah, that's okay. Once they see how good I do, they'll want me back. Especially when the fever passes and all the rich folks come back to stay." Eager to depart, now that they needed him, William scooped his rod off the ground and reeled it in.

"Whoo-ee!" A foot-long white bass dangled on the end of the line, caught when William had all but given up.

"Whoa!" Dennis said, stepping alongside for a closer look. "String that thing up, and let's go. I can almost taste it."

"What happened to 'this is private property'?" William smirked, ready to toss the fish back.

"Not so fast." Dennis threw an arm in front of William. "The groundskeeper gave us permission—just for today. You didn't give me a chance to get it all out."

Fish for breakfast then. William couldn't wait.

Ma sat on the front porch in her wooden rocker, a light shawl around her shoulders and William's three-year-old brother lying in her lap. Her black shoe, worn near-bare at the sole, tapped the floorboards, creating a creak-squeak-crack rhythm as the chair moved forward and back, forward and back.

Her lips tight and her brows drawn together, she didn't seem to notice Dennis and William's approach.

"Hey, Ma! Caught us some breakfast!" William called as he mounted the porch steps from the rutted dirt street.

Ma's gaze sharpened as she focused on her sons and then the fish dangling from the line. A hint of a smile graced her lips and her shoulders relaxed.

William's chest puffed with pride, grateful that he'd been able to ease her burden, even if only for one meager meal.

"Saints be praised," Ma said, shifting the little boy higher against her chest. "Clean that fish and give it to Rosie to bake, will ya'?"

"Good morning, Ma," Dennis said, clapping William on the back and taking the fish from him.

Ma nodded, her smile slipping a bit. The silver crucifix on her rosary beads dangled from the pocket of her apron, and she patted the pocket, shoving the beads inside.

Elated and eager to tell her that not only had he caught breakfast, but that he had a job at the club for the weekend, William grabbed the cane chair from the opposite side of the porch and began dragging it toward Ma, the chair legs stuttering over the uneven boards.

Ma held a hand out, palm facing him. "Stay there, William."

The chair legs ceased their clamoring, and William stood still, examining Ma and trying to decipher why she'd held him at bay.

"Not too close." Her gaze dropped to his little brother, and William took stock of him for the first time.

Face flushed. Eyes a bit glassy. A red rash peeking out from above his open collar. He seemed to strain to swallow and then sobbed softly, rubbing his face against Ma's dress.

William's chest tightened. The symptoms were there. Same as his sister Anne had only two years ago. No wonder Ma's voice had been so stern and those beads were slipping from her pocket again.

Scarlet fever.

Most every house on the block had one, two, or even three kids sick with it over the past weeks. The Cook household had been spared. Until now.

The little boy would recover in a week, most likely. The fever would break, the rash would disappear, maybe leaving peeling skin in its wake, and his brother would be wreaking havoc on his siblings once again.

That's how it was supposed to be with Anne. But Anne's rash hadn't given way. Her knees ached and she grew weak, barely leaving her bed.

A memory flashed in William's mind of Anne crossing the tawny late-winter grass in their small backyard, eager to join their sisters Ellen, Bridget, and Margaret in skipping rope, but being so winded at the exertion that she'd collapsed against the old pear tree and slid to the ground. William had darted inside, yelling for Ma and Pa . . .

He shivered, trying to shake off the dread pitting in his stomach. This would be different. Pretty Anne, freckles covering every inch of her face, had always been sickly, the first one in the house to catch whatever was going around.

"He's got the fever, doesn't he?" William's voice, which tended to squeak and croak often these days, came out downright gravelly.

Ma nodded, her eyes welling with tears. "Started last evening. He had a fitful night. His throat and head must be hurting something awful." She stroked his strawberry blonde hair, pushing the wavy locks from his clammy forehead.

William stepped back, dragging the chair with him. This time, the rumble of a creamery wagon rolling down the street, its milk bottles rattling, drowned out the sound. The odor of burning wood with a touch of sulfur rolled in on a wave of morning air.

It wouldn't do for him to get sick. Nor Dennis or Rose, but they were older and likely wouldn't catch it. If the men at the club knew that his little brother was sick, would they even want him to work guiding guests into the boats?

William wouldn't get sick. He couldn't.

He returned the chair to its spot, his mood dampened, if not drowned. "You need anything, Ma? Want me to bring you out some of that fish I caught?"

Ma smiled. "That sounds delicious. Make sure Rosie cooks it up the way we like it, with lots of butter."

He grinned. He and Ma shared a love of butter. "Butter makes it better," she always said.

She'd taken Anne's death the hardest. Then buried Pa not six months later. She had to be worried now. Had to be quaking inside. But she didn't show it. Ma was stronger than anyone he knew, with a faith deeper than anyone he knew, except maybe Father McGuire.

She leaned on her faith in times of sickness. She had to.

They all did.

That afternoon, Dennis grabbed one end of a wooden canoe and William the other, and they carried it across the lawn toward the lake where four other canoes sat, ready for William to wipe them clean in preparation for the guests.

Dennis dusted his hands on his pants and glanced toward the clubhouse and then at the sky. "I best be heading up there. Some folks'll probably need help with their bags and such."

William squinted into the sun, shading his brow with a hand. "Do they bring lots of stuff? It's only two days, and they're only coming from Pittsburgh."

Examining his shoes for grass and leaves that might be sticking to them, Dennis shrugged. "Some do. You'd be surprised at all the fine things they like to bring along. Milliner's boxes and all that frou-frou." He wrinkled his nose, but William had noticed Dennis taking more interest in that so-called "frou-frou" lately. Especially when it was worn by pretty blonde girls like Mary Donnelly, who lived three doors down from them.

The sun blistered by late afternoon, and William wiped sweat from his brow with his sleeve as he sat watching fancily dressed men and women coming and going between the cottages and the clubhouse. He wished some of them would take a turn around the lake. Maybe if he could get out on a boat, he could cool off. He stared hungrily at the water lapping against the shoreline, tempted to take a dip.

He lay back on the grass, crossed his feet at the ankles, and closed his eyes. His little brother had been at the forefront of his thoughts all day. Was he feeling better? Had the rash faded or was it getting worse? Likely worse since he'd only been showing symptoms for a day.

A splash sounded further down the shore, and opening his eyes, William caught a blue heron flying overhead, its long legs dragging as it flapped its wings and crossed the lake.

"Are you the man I see about a turn in the canoe?"

The gentleman's voice came from behind, startling William. He bolted upright, then scrambled to his feet. "Yes, sir," he stammered, straightening his clothes and giving the nearest canoe a quick visual inspection.

"Great. I'd like to take one out." The man, probably a little older than Rose, spoke with a German accent. "I'm guessing this place looks even prettier from the water than it does from land."

"Yes, sir. It's something to see, for sure." He dumped a paddle into the boat and began dragging it to the drop-in point.

To his surprise, the man grabbed the other end and lifted.

"I've got this," William said. "You don't have to do anything." He looked the man up and down. His clothes, while neat and tidy, didn't look near as formal or as expensive as the suits the other, older men wore.

"Nonsense. Why should you do all the work?"

Because I'm being paid to, William thought but didn't say out loud.

They dropped the boat at the edge of the water, and the man held out his hand. "I'm Josef. Josef Meyer. What's your name?"

William wasn't sure how to answer. Not because he didn't know his own name but because this interaction was so unexpected. "Uh, William." He stared at Josef's proffered hand, unsure whether he should shake it. "William Cook."

Josef smiled then reached farther, grasping William's hand in a firm shake. "Don't be timid, young fellow. I'm not one of them." He tilted his head toward the clubhouse, grinning.

"But you're a guest here," William said, knowing that neither he nor anyone he typically brushed shoulders with could gain entry to the club by any way but a servants' entrance.

"Yes, for two days at the tail end of a season in which everyone's been scared back to the city because of an epidemic of scarlet fever. What does that tell you about how I rank?" Josef laughed as he stepped into the lake, the water sloshing over his shoe.

At the words "scarlet fever," William tensed. What if Josef knew William's little brother was home sick with the fever this very minute? And that not only William, but his siblings Rose and Dennis mingled among the servants and guests here at the club?

"I'm the son of a low man on the totem pole," Josef said,

his accent particularly thick on the last words. "I thank you for your help, and I'll be back in after I take a jaunt around the lake. Is there anything special I should look for?"

William worked to focus on Josef's question, tossing aside his worries for the time being. "Uh, there's a muskrat that had babies over there." He pointed to the far end of the lake. "You might smell her if you get close enough."

Josef nodded. "Thank you, William. I'll see you in a bit." He doffed his hat, set one foot in the bottom of the canoe, and shoved off with the other.

William held his breath until the man safely paddled out a dozen or so yards. His first encounter with a guest had gone fine, as far as he could tell.

A couple of hours later, William rose as he glimpsed Josef paddling toward him. The sun had sunk deeper in the sky, but the temperature hadn't dropped as he'd hoped. If anything, it'd increased. His poor little brother; how could he fight a fever in this heat?

Josef dug his paddle into the dirt then hopped from the canoe as if he'd done it a million times before. "Good afternoon, William." He dragged the canoe ashore as William scrambled to help him.

It'd be just William's luck that a club member would spot him standing by while a guest did the work. They'd summarily dismiss him as lazy and shiftless.

Sweat soaked the back of Josef's shirt and made dark circles on the fabric beneath his arms as he gave the canoe a final shove. "I smelled your muskrat," he said, a cheerful lilt to his German accent, "but I didn't spot her."

"She's a bit shy, but a crust of bread does the trick in drawing her out." On numerous mornings, all of William's bread crusts went to the chubby rodent, leaving him nothing for fish bait.

"I'll have to remember that when I return." Josef reached into one pocket, then the other, and handed William a couple of coins. "For your trouble," he said.

Trouble? Josef himself had done the work. Of course, in between his departure and return, William had taken two young ladies out in the rowboat, driving against the breeze toward the cove they wanted to investigate. His arms ached from the effort already—and they hadn't even tipped him!

"Thank you, Mr. Meyer." William couldn't keep the smile from his face as he fingered the coins, slipping them through his fingers and then into his own pocket.

"I've got to get to the clubhouse. There's a lovely *fräulein* working there whom I don't want to miss. *Danke.*" He winked and trotted toward the nearest cottage, probably to change before supper.

Could the *"fraulein"* be Rose? Nah. A bevy of girls from his neighborhood worked there. It could be any one of them. Though Josef seemed gentlemanly enough to court his prim sister.

As William stooped to grab the canoe, his gaze caught on a small object jutting out of the mud. From the edge of the water, he plucked a greenish-brown stone only an inch or so wide bearing no resemblance to the sandstone, coal, or shale he found when hunting for skipping stones.

Using his thumb, he rubbed the mud from it, flipped it over, and examined it, noticing now some swirls and streaks of brown intermixed with the dull green. He rotated it back and forth between his fingers. "Hey," he said to nobody, "kinda like a three-leaf clover." And he slid his thumb over what looked like three leaves and a stubby stem.

"William!" Dennis called from across the lawn. "Ready to walk home?"

He hadn't realized it'd grown so late, but Dennis had told him he'd come by when he was done for the day, which was the same time William was to replace the boats beneath the shelter and go home. He pocketed the rock and turned his attention back to the canoe. "Yeah, just let me put this canoe away."

On the way back to South Fork, William fingered the coins in his pocket, his heart swelling with pride at his tip. If only there were some salve, some tincture, some ointment he could buy that would heal his little brother, but the only known cure for scarlet fever seemed to be time, rest, and drinking ample liquids.

His fingers bumped against the other object in his pocket—the shamrock stone. Given the coins he'd gotten just before he'd discovered it, he wondered if it might be a lucky object. Pa had said that luck was nonsense; God's providence was the only "luck" one needed. Still, the rock seemed special to him somehow.

"Hey, look what I found," William said, holding the stone for Dennis to see.

"Let me see that."

William handed it over, and Dennis fingered the stone, flipping it over in his hand and tossing it lightly. "Where'd you get this?"

"Found it on the ground by the canoe after a guest got out." He snatched it from Dennis and pocketed it, leery of Dennis's accusatory tone.

"And did you find this guest to see if it belonged to him or her?" Dennis kept moving, kicking stones from his path as they turned a street corner, but William could feel his stare.

"No. He'd left already, and I don't even know if it was his. Coulda' been there a long time." Unlikely though, considering it was lying on top of the mud and not buried in it. He probably should've guessed it belonged to Josef and chased after him. Now that he thought about it, he *had* rummaged through his pockets for those coins he'd given him. The rock could've dropped then.

"You oughta' take it tomorrow and see if it belongs to him."

William sighed, knowing Dennis was right but not liking the fact. Either fact, really—Dennis being right *and* possibly handing back the rock that fit so well in his hands and in his pocket.

"It's just a rock, you know," Dennis said, bumping him with his shoulder, which was supposed to encourage him or something, he guessed.

"I'll do it," William said. "I won't like it, but I'll do it."

The next day, dragonflies flitted across the water, and a pair of goldfinches fluttered in the low-hanging limbs of a giant sycamore tree as William scanned the lake and then the path running between the lake and the clubhouse.

The sun hung overhead, obscured by a few puffy clouds, when Josef approached the drop-in point. The tantalizing aroma of meat cooking over a fire drifted on the breeze.

William stood from his vantage point in the shade and hurried to grab the right-sized paddle for the tall man. He waved at Josef, but a nervous sensation in his belly made him wish the kind German had decided to forego paddling the lake today.

"William, how are you today?" Josef asked, a smile lighting his face, emphasizing the redness of his nose and cheeks. Looked like he'd gotten a bit too much sun yesterday.

"I'm good," William said, handing the paddle over. "I, uh . . ." He reached into his pocket and rubbed his thumb over the smooth stone, his heart unreasonably achy at simply returning a dumb rock.

"Yes, William?" Josef waited, his eyes wide in expectation.

"I, uh, I found this stone on the ground yesterday after you left," he said, pulling the green-brown rock from his pocket. "Does it belong to you?"

Josef's gaze traveled to William's palm, and his expression softened. He sunk a hand into one of his pants pockets and then the other, coming up with nothing. "Yes," he said, plucking the stone from William's hand. "I didn't even know I'd lost it." He tossed the stone back and forth from hand to hand, seemingly lost in thought.

"Thank you for returning it to me. I appreciate it. It's . . . special. One of my brothers—he's studying to be a priest—came across this stone quite by chance. Across the Atlantic, if you can believe it." He lifted his eyes to William. "And then," he said, offering the stone back to him, "it passed to me. I think maybe you could use it right now."

A smile spread across William's face. Josef was giving it back? "Golly, thank you, Mr. Meyer. Are you sure?"

"It's just a rock," he said, shrugging. "And yet . . ." His eyes held a faraway look. "There's a legend connecting it to an Irish saint. They say it belonged to Saint Patrick himself." Josef slid his thumb across the rock, hesitated, touched it gently to his chest, right over his heart, and then handed it over, his eyes shining. "Yes, you take it."

"*Danke,*" William spouted, mimicking Josef's expression of thanks the day before.

Josef nodded, grinned, and shoved off onto the lake, a songbird in a nearby tree whistling its farewell.

William woke before dawn the next morning to his little brother's crying. Crying was a regular occurrence in a household with so many young children, and he typically slept through it, but he'd been on edge when he climbed into bed last night after Ma confided in the four oldest children that their little brother had not improved yet. His fever had climbed higher, his rash had grown brighter, and his tongue remained covered in white.

At least none of the other children had gotten it. *Yet*.

He dressed quietly so as not to wake Dennis and padded down the stairs, relieved to get away from the stuffy heat of the upstairs room that had only a small window to draw in nighttime air.

Downstairs, Ma paced the kitchen with his little brother on her hip. A kettle sat atop the woodstove, emitting a cloud of steam. The morning sun crept in the eastern-facing window, casting light over the dull room and its occupants.

Circles hung beneath Ma's eyes, and stray hairs escaped the bun sitting askew on the back of her head.

His brother's tear-stained cheeks shone red. He wore only an undergarment, and the rash on his chest, arms, and legs contrasted with the paler patches of flesh. Around his elbows and knees, deep red lines rimmed the folds of his skin.

William's heart beat heavy in his chest. His little brother had to recover. *He had to*. He wasn't Anne. He wouldn't get rheumatic fever too. He wouldn't die. *Please, God, no*.

He knew the answer without even asking but asked anyway. "Is he any better?"

Ma shook her head, her eyes watery.

William's mouth grew dry, and he swallowed with difficulty.

His brother's head lolled onto Ma's shoulder, and she spoke softly. "Once he falls asleep, I'll put him to bed.

Maybe he'll sleep for a while." She paced toward the picture window at the front of the house and gazed into the empty street. "Remember him at Holy Mass this morning."

"I will, Ma," he whispered. "I will."

William took the stairs by twos, knocked on his sisters' door to wake them, then returned to his room to wake Dennis. While Dennis moved through his typical morning routine of grumbling, rolling over, and pulling the covers over his head, William walked to his own bed and slid his hand beneath the indented pillow that still held the shape of his head.

Last night, before bed, not sure where else to put it, he'd placed the shamrock stone there. Furtively, before Dennis roused, he tiptoed to his brother's little bed and drew down the covers.

He rubbed the stone between his hands, blew on it to warm it with his breath, kissed it, and then slid it beneath the pillow, a silent but desperate prayer for healing on his lips.

Two hours later, the Cook family, minus Ma and their youngest sibling, tromped down the concrete steps outside of church. They'd stayed late after Mass, kneeling in their pew and praying for their little brother as Ma had requested. William had offered his Communion for his healing. Of course, he'd done the same for Anne, and she'd still died.

Even so, her death hadn't been God's fault, according to

Ma. It simply hadn't been His will to heal her for reasons neither he, nor Ma, nor Pa, nor any of his family could understand. "Have faith," Ma had said. "God knows best what each of us needs." William had accepted her answer, even if it rankled him. How could Anne's death have been best for anyone?

They walked home without the usual hullabaloo that surrounded the seven—today, six—siblings walking, talking, laughing, and chasing each other, eager to reach home and a hot breakfast made special on Sunday by Ma.

When they neared the house, William raced ahead of the others, eager to see how his little brother fared. Had he slept? Had the fever lessened or the rash faded? Had he grown weak, like Anne had? No, it would be too soon for that, wouldn't it?

The wooden door swung open on a gust of air and slammed against the interior wall. William groped for the knob, anticipating a scolding from Ma. No scolding came.

Ma sat in the parlor, mid-morning light bathing her in a golden halo. In her hand she squeezed one of Pa's handkerchiefs and pressed it to her face, dabbing one eye and then the other. A sob choked her as she watched William, then the others, file through the open door.

Rose rushed to her, falling on her knees and clutching Ma's skirt. "What's happened? Where—is he okay?" Always sure and steady of voice, the anguish in Rose's voice nearly broke William.

Dennis's hand came over his shoulder, squeezing lightly.

They held their collective breaths, waiting for Ma's response when their younger brother raced into the room from the kitchen, a soft leather ball clutched in his small hand. A giant smile grew on his face as he beheld his siblings gathered together. Gripping the ball tighter, he launched it at William, hitting him in the shin.

Gone was the red rash around his neck. His once-flushed face glowed its healthy, natural shade. And his green eyes shone clear and alert.

Joy bubbled from Ma as much as words. "He's well. He's completely well. No fever, no rash. I put him to bed ill, and he woke hale and hearty with a twinkle in his eye."

"Oh, Ma!" Rose clung to Ma's skirts, happy tears trailing down her cheeks.

The other children crowded around their little brother, squeezing him with hugs and covering him with kisses.

William picked up the ball to return it. "Here you go, bud," he said, holding the ball out.

Instead of accepting it, the little boy held out a fist, a mischievous smile lighting his face.

"What do you have there?" Maybe he wanted to make a trade for the ball.

The little fist opened, and there sat William's shamrock stone.

His heart tripping, William crouched to his brother's level. "Where did you get this?" He must've discovered it under his pillow.

"Patrick found it!" he said, pointing to himself, his voice gleeful. He prodded William's closed hand.

William offered Patrick his palm, and Patrick dropped the shamrock stone in it, then snatched the ball and raced around the room, his youngest sisters trailing behind him.

"I thought you were gonna give that back," Dennis said, peering over William's shoulder at the shamrock stone.

"I tried. Mr. Meyer said he thought I could use it." William shrugged, struggling to make sense of what had happened to cure Patrick so suddenly and whether the unusual rock had anything to do with it. How could it? And yet . . . Josef had said it was "special."

"Mr. Meyer?" Rose appeared suddenly beside them, curiosity and interest alight in her eyes. "I met him at the clubhouse. A kind German man from Pittsburgh, yes?"

William nodded, confident now that Rose was the lovely *fräulein* who'd caught Josef's eye.

"What is it?" Ma asked from her seat, her eyes dry now.

"Just a stone I found," William said, extending it to Ma.

Ma traced the crude leaves and the stubby stem. "This," she said, her finger caressing the shamrock stone, "and the many prayers and Communions you offered"—she looked at each of them in turn and then to Patrick, who rushed to her lap and climbed up—"delivered us a wee miracle, I think."

She pressed a kiss to Patrick's forehead.

William reclaimed the shamrock stone and tucked it into his pocket for safe-keeping. His heart swelled with gratitude to a God so good he'd restored Patrick to good health. And to Josef: *danke*.

"Danke" is set in historical Johnstown, Pennsylvania, in and around South Fork and the South Fork Fishing and Hunting Club, a summertime resort frequented by industrialist tycoons such as Andrew Carnegie, Henry Clay Frick, and Andrew Mellon. Just months after this story takes place, the dam creating Lake Conemaugh gave way, sending 3.6 billion gallons of water hurtling fourteen miles down the Little Conemaugh River, destroying nearly everything in its path and killing more than 2,000 people. A novel set during the Great Johnstown Flood has been brewing in my imagination for years. Josef and Rose are its central characters.

ABOUT THE AUTHOR

CAROLYN ASTFALK writes from the sweetest place on Earth, Hershey, Pennsylvania, where she lives with her husband and four children. In addition to her contemporary Catholic romances (sometimes referred to as Theology of the Body fiction), including the young adult coming-of-age story *Rightfully Ours*, she is a Catholicmom.com contributor. She is a member of the Catholic Writers Guild and Pennwriters. When she is not washing dishes, doing laundry, or reading, you can find her blogging about books, faith, and family life at www.CarolynAstfalk.com.

Present Day,
The Midwest, USA

6

GRACE AMONG GANGSTERS

by Leslea Wahl

Luke follows his two younger siblings as they march down the hall to Grandma's condo. When their mom had mentioned to them over breakfast that it would be nice for them to swing by Grandma's some time that day, all three teens collectively groaned. Not that they don't enjoy spending time with their grandmother . . . but middle-of-the-week visits are difficult.

As they near the door, Luke tries to improve his attitude. But with a looming college decision hovering over him like an impending dark cloud of doom, he's in no mood for lighthearted chit-chat. However, the three siblings had made a pact—sports practices, club meetings, homework, and contemplating major life decisions all took a backseat to Grandma.

Austin raps on her front door, tapping out a rhythm with his knuckles like he's four instead of fourteen.

"Happy Saint Patrick's Day!" he hollers as soon as Grandma opens the door.

She's wearing one of her many sweatsuits. Today's choice is festive green.

"Thank you for making the time to come by!" Her youngest grandson towers over her, but she draws him in for a hug anyway.

Celia holds up the floral arrangement they'd grabbed at the grocery store—an explosion of green carnations, white roses, delicate baby's breath, and greenery. The bouquet is spiked with festive jeweled shamrocks that catch the light as they bend and sway with every movement. "Of course. We know how much you love holidays."

"These are beautiful!" Grandma accepts the flowers and closes her eyes as she breathes in their scent. She then links her free arm through Celia's, and the two of them precede Luke and Austin into the condo. "How's the driving going?"

Luke's sister tucks a long strand of brown hair behind her ear. "Great! I should be ready to get my license in a few weeks."

"Wonderful." Grandma glances at Luke. "And have you made a decision about college?"

"Not yet." Luke turns to shut the door. The perfect excuse to hide his annoyance. The extra pressure from everyone isn't making the decision any easier. He turns back and claps his hands. Time to fake some enthusiasm. "So, who's ready to bake?"

"Let's get to it!" Grandma leads the way to the kitchen.

While she places the flowers in a vase, the siblings wash their hands then perch on stools around the kitchen island, the requisite baking sheet and rolling pin in front of each of them.

Grandma opens the refrigerator to pull out a bowl of cookie dough. "I really am glad you're here. I know you're all incredibly busy, so I wasn't sure you'd have the time."

"Absolutely. We couldn't break tradition." Austin dips a sneaky finger into the bowl to steal a little dough. He pops the small bit into his mouth before Grandma can bat his hand away.

Ever since Luke can remember, Grandma has celebrated holidays with them by making and decorating sugar cookies, whether it be Thanksgiving, Christmas, Valentine's Day, Saint Patrick's Day, Easter, or the Fourth of July. Her supply of holiday cookie cutters probably puts most bakeries to shame.

He takes in Grandma's wide smile, suddenly glad they'd agreed to come. He felt a little guilty that they'd stopped helping bake the cookies for a few years, using their busy schedules as an excuse. But after their recent summer vacation to the Southwest with Grandma and their parents, the siblings decided they should restart the tradition. The catalyst to change their minds: Grandma won't be around forever.

Luke grabs a hunk of dough to start rolling out. "Dad said Saint Patrick's Day is your favorite holiday. Is that true?" Seems like an odd favorite.

Grandma reaches for the shamrock-shaped cookie

cutter. "Well, it's certainly near the top."

"You're part Irish, right?" Celia sifts through the pile of metal shapes.

"Yes, my father's family all came from Ireland generations ago." Grandma runs her index finger along the smooth clover shape in her hand. "But that's not really why the holiday means so much to me."

Luke sets down his rolling pin. Something in Grandma's voice makes him look up. Celia and Austin must also hear the slight tease in her tone because they stop what they're doing and glance at each other.

That sly grin of hers—the one they all first noticed over the summer—clued him in. "Something you want to tell us, Grandma?"

"Story time!" The teens say in unison, a bit louder than desired for inside voices.

Grandma laughs. "Well, there is a story I've never told you . . . something that happened to me when I was eleven and my brother Harry was thirteen. Every Saint Patrick's Day, I'm reminded of that experience." She picks up her rolling pin and begins flattening a ball of dough. "As you know, my father was a professor of archeology at a college in Iowa. It was in 1957. Our father's break between terms fell in the middle of March. My mother was away taking care of her parents while Harry and I stayed home with our father. His plan for the week was to finally tackle a few projects around the house while we were at school."

Grandma draws a deep breath. A smile lifts the corners of her lips as she launches into her Saint Patrick's Day tale.

1957

Having Daddy in charge is a little odd. In the afternoons when Harry and I normally complete our schoolwork, he's usually still at the university or cooped up in his den working on lesson plans or grading papers. Mama typically makes us a snack while we tell her about our day. But with her gone for the week and Daddy banging away down the hall, installing some shelves in the closet, we're forced to fend for ourselves. Before settling down to start our work, I find two apples in the refrigerator and offer one to Harry, but he apparently prefers eating peanut butter right out of the jar. If only Mama could see that!

Since he's off work this week, I suppose I could insist that Daddy make us a proper snack and sit with us. But he seems to like finding out about our day over supper—a meal he pulls out of the freezer and warms up in the oven. I guess Mama thought we might starve to death if we had to rely on Daddy remembering to cook. Last week when she was preparing all those extra meals, I thought she was being a little overzealous, but seeing how our snack time is going—looks like she was right. There's not enough peanut butter in the cupboard to feed us for a whole week.

Without our usual routine, or maybe because of Daddy's constant banging, I can't seem to focus. How are we to do our schoolwork with all that racket? Harry hunches over his math book, his loose-leaf paper spread across the kitchen table, as if not affected at all by the noise. How does he do that? He's always so calm, cool, and collected. While I'm . . . well, not.

Reluctantly, I pull my spelling word list from my school bag. Mama usually helps quiz me on the words, making a fun game out of it. How will I pass my spelling test without her? I'm sure neither Daddy nor Harry will help the way Mama does. What a disaster. Things just don't run smoothly without her here.

I open my notebook and write the first word on the list in my best cursive. Maybe I can at least get extra marks for my penmanship. I've just started to write a sentence using the word when the telephone on the wall rings.

The incessant pounding stops. Daddy's footsteps pad down the hallway to the front room.

"Hello. Turner residence. Mac speaking."

I wait. Maybe it's Mama calling to ask about our day.

"Oh, hi, Joe. Good to hear from you."

Not Mama. I focus on my sentence again.

"No kidding? Well, welcome to the Midwest."

Somehow, I mess up my capital L. My loops never look pretty enough. I turn my pencil upside down and start erasing the letter.

"Kansas City? It's a few hours from here."

I brush away the bits of eraser and try again.

"No. I'd love to see you, but I can't get away."

The loops of my second try are slightly better. How does Mrs. Hamilton make the letters so perfect?

"My wife's away taking care of her parents, so I've got the kids this week."

I lean sideways, trying to get a glimpse of Daddy in the living room.

"No, not so little anymore. Harry is thirteen, and Gracie just turned eleven."

Who is this Joe person?

"No. I couldn't. They're in school this week."

I kick Harry's leg with my saddle shoe, return his glare, and nod toward the living room. Daddy's talking about us; the least we can do is listen.

"I mean, I guess they could miss a week of school, but why? What is so important at this site?"

Harry's eyes narrow. Now he's interested.

"You can't tell me more than that?"

I hold my breath, not willing to miss a thing.

"Yeah, I know you'd never insist if it wasn't important. But the timing's not good." Daddy lets out a deep breath. "Well, let me think about it. How can I reach you?"

The faint scratch of pencil against paper reaches my straining ears.

"Okay. I'll get back to you. Good-bye." Silence follows, disrupted only by the distinct rattle of the handset landing on the base, followed by footsteps heading back down the hallway.

I lean toward Harry. "What do you think that was about?"

Harry shrugs. "I don't know, but I have a feeling we'll be missing a few days of school. When has he ever turned down fieldwork?"

Harry's right. The exciting lure of a new find is always

too enticing for Daddy to resist. Mama loves to tell the story of how their honeymoon to Florida was cut short, and they spent the rest of their first week of marriage in Louisiana at an archeological site.

Fine with me. At least it will get me out of taking this spelling test.

We pull up alongside the other cars parked in front of a white, two-story home with a large front porch. Three men standing out front stop their conversation and watch us. Daddy opens the door of our Chevy and gets out of the car. Harry and I do the same. The drive from our home in Iowa to this small town outside of Kansas City took a few hours, and I'm ready to stretch my legs. Daddy places his hat on his slicked-back dark hair and smooths out his cardigan.

One of the men grins. He drops his cigarette, twisting it in the dirt with the toe of his brown dress shoe, then walks toward us. He reaches out to shake hands with Daddy. "Mac, good to see you."

Daddy shakes with his right hand and pats the man's shoulder with his left. "Joe, it's great to see you."

Joe turns to his colleagues. "Gentlemen, this is my good buddy, Mackenzie Turner."

The men all shake hands and finish their introductions, then Daddy presents us. "These are my children, Harry and Grace." He adjusts the brim of his hat. "Okay, Joe. You have thoroughly piqued my curiosity. Now that we're here, what's your big discovery?"

Joe grins. "Right this way." He rolls up his shirt sleeves as he walks up the steps.

We follow Daddy and Joe into the house. Nothing stands out. Just an ordinary home in an ordinary small town—except maybe for the piles of boxes lining the walls of the front room. An old Victrola radio on a table next to a floral armchair are the only furnishings in sight. Reminds me of my grandmother's parlor.

Joe stops inside the living room. "The homeowner recently passed away, and the daughter has decided to sell the property." He pats a stack of boxes. "She and her husband have been cleaning out the house and came across something unusual."

He motions for us to follow him down a narrow hallway. At the end, a bright light shines on a brick wall. Or at least what's left of the wall. The center bricks have been chipped away, creating a rough archway.

Daddy stops and runs a hand along the bricks. He looks at Joe with raised eyebrows. "Okay, this is interesting."

Joe nods. "This wall was hidden by a large armoire. When the daughter and her husband moved it, they found this bricked-in doorway. Naturally, they wondered what lay behind it."

Joe ducks and squeezes through the passageway. Daddy follows, disappearing from view. Harry and I scurry after them. The bright light illuminates a stone stairwell. I keep one hand on the rough wall as I follow Harry down the steep stone steps. The narrow staircase takes a right turn then continues down another flight.

Before I reach the bottom of the stairs, Daddy's low whistle reaches my ears. I emerge into a large stone room. More bright lights are set up throughout the space, revealing a dozen or so round tables and stacks of chairs pushed to the sides of the room. A huge, dark wooden counter takes up one entire wall.

"A speakeasy?" Daddy wanders around the room, examining everything with narrow-eyed intrigue.

Joe looks quite pleased with himself. "It would appear so."

I lean toward Harry. "What's a speakeasy?"

His eyes widen. "I learned about them last year when our history class was talking about the 1920s. During the prohibition years, alcohol was illegal, so mobsters created hidden taverns."

My mouth drops open. Mobsters? Good gravy!

Daddy finishes his initial sweep around the room. "Well, this is certainly a fascinating find, but I'm still not sure why you wanted me to see it in person."

"Because of this." Joe walks toward a large open crate about the size of my bed.

There's more? I glance at Harry. His eyes reflect the same excitement that's speeding up my heartbeat. We join the two men, who are peering into the crate. Daddy slowly examines the contents—a mishmash of paintings, sculptures, and various other large and small items.

Joe hands him a document. "This was inside."

Daddy's forehead creases as he studies it. The moment recognition hits, his face transforms.

His head whips toward Joe. "The Sultana?"

Joe offers a toothy grin. "Yes. Can you believe it, Mac? After all these years, we finally have proof of our theory."

After checking into the small inn down the block, we meet Joe for supper. Harry and I hope to hear the rest of the story. We'd peppered Daddy with a million questions after leaving the house, but he just said he'd explain later.

The two of us sit patiently as the two old friends catch up on their lives. I shift in my seat—enough of the boring stuff. Come on, get to the story.

Once we place our food order with Mrs. Murphy—the owner of the inn, whose red curls make her look like Lucille Ball—our excruciating wait is finally over.

Joe turns to look at Harry and me. "I'm sure you kids have a lot of questions."

I nod. "Yes, who's the Sultana?" Sounds awfully exotic. Harry and I have been trying to figure it out all afternoon. All kinds of possibilities swirl through our brains. My best guess is that the Sultana is a mysterious rich woman from a foreign country. Harry pictures an illusionist like Houdini.

Daddy places his hands on the table. "The Sultana was a steamship."

Disappointment tugs at my heart. A steamship? That's not exciting at all.

Joe chuckles, his gaze on my expression. "After the Civil War, the Sultana was dispatched to take soldiers home. She was heading up the Mississippi River, traveling from

Mississippi to St. Louis." His eyes widen. "But she never reached her destination. The Sultana sank near Memphis."

Daddy leans forward. "Actually, it remains the worst maritime disaster in U.S. history."

"Worse than the Titanic?" Harry asks.

Daddy nods. "Yes. More people died in the Sultana sinking."

Wow. But . . . "What does that have to do with the talk-easy?"

Joe chuckles again. "Speakeasy."

"That's a great question, Grace," Daddy says. "One I'd love to hear the answer to as well."

The conversation comes to a halt when Mrs. Murphy delivers our food. Joe digs into his meal but stops and waits patiently while Harry, Daddy, and I say our prayers.

I'm anxious to hear more of the story, but my companions are more concerned with consuming their meals. How frustrating. Discoveries are waiting to be made, and mysteries need to be uncovered. Harry nudges me with his knee to stop my tapping foot. My brother's patience never ceases to amaze me.

Finally, Joe takes a sip of water, then wipes his mouth with his napkin. He looks my way and winks. The anticipation has twisted my insides into a knot of anxiousness, and I'm pretty sure Joe knows it and is enjoying my turmoil. He leans back. "The house down the road once belonged to Eddie Manzanelli."

Daddy sets his fork down. "Eddie the Bull?"

Who the heck is Eddie the Bull?

Joe nods, a satisfied smirk on his face.

Harry dips a French fry into his ketchup. How can he eat at a time like this?

Daddy glances at me like he's not sure he wants to say anything more in front of me. I want to beg, but if I act like a little kid, he'll never share the story. So, I pick up my fork and swirl it through my spaghetti, pretending to be as unconcerned as Harry.

I guess the strategy worked, because he starts talking. "Eddie the Bull was one of the trusted advisors to the mobster Sugarhouse Pete."

What is with these names? They sound like characters from Harry's comic books.

"Pete DiGiovanni happened to be a collector of historical artifacts," Joe tells us.

Daddy leans back. "That explains a lot."

What? Does he have a screw loose? That explains nothing!

Daddy and Joe huddle together, practically talking over each other. I look at Harry. He knows me well and shakes his head no. I know I should listen. I really do. I ought to be patient and wait for the men to bring us back into the conversation, but I just can't do it.

"What's so special about the Sultana?"

Harry sighs and closes his eyes. Joe and Daddy stare at me. In my head, my mother's voice scolds me for my rude outburst. *Grace Elizabeth Turner, you need to show some manners, young lady!*

I wait for my father's stern rebuke, but instead, Joe

elbows Daddy. "Mac, she's got your fiery passion."

Daddy chuckles. "And my patience . . . or lack thereof."

Harry nudges me with his knee again. This time the silent message is positive: *You are one lucky girl!*

I make a mental note to tell Father O'Brien about disrespecting my elders during my next Confession.

Joe claps his hands together. "Okay. Here's the story. One summer, years ago, your father and I were working on a dig site along the banks of the Mississippi. As we unearthed Indian artifacts, we got to talking about the Sultana. You see, the boat was carrying home more than the soldiers. She was also loaded with precious items being sent to St. Louis for safe-keeping until things settled down after the war."

"Tensions were quite high after the Civil War ended." Daddy pushes away his plate. "Many museums, churches, and private collectors gathered important items and sent them out West to be protected until things settled down in the war-torn states."

Joe reaches for his water glass. "A manifest existed of the items, but after the ship sank, many were never recovered."

"They're at the bottom of the river?" Harry asks.

Daddy rubs his jaw. "Yes, that was the theory. However, rumors suggested that some items made it off the ship."

Whoa, Nellie. "And that's what you believed?"

Joe snaps his fingers and points at me. "You got it. We thought maybe the items were still out there somewhere.

Your dad and I looked into some of the theories but never found any promising leads."

Daddy shakes his head. "And somehow, the DiGiovanni family came into possession of the items."

"We'll probably never know how that happened, but I'm guessing that when the feds started swarming Kansas City and closed in on the family's operation, Eddie took the items to his 'establishment' down the road here, for safe-keeping."

I pick up my milkshake, satisfied. Lost artifacts, a sunken ship, a mob family. I can't wait to tell Mama.

Harry's vibrating snores wake me the next morning. I provide a wake-up call of my own by throwing my pillow at his head, which jerks him wide awake.

"Good morning." I smile sweetly.

"Yeah," he murmurs through his yawn.

I climb out of bed and find a note from Daddy on the dresser.

I'm over at the house. Come on by after you have breakfast.

He's probably been up for hours. Daddy can never get his projects out of his mind.

We dress and clamber down the stairs to the restaurant. Mrs. Murphy waves at us as we slide into a booth by the front window.

"Good morning, you two." She sets two glasses of orange juice on our table. "I promised your daddy that I would get you fed. So, two specials coming up."

"Thank you." My mouth waters in anticipation. Last

night's dinner was delicious—once I finally got around to eating it. "Would it be possible to order a cup of cocoa as well?"

"Sure thing, sweetheart." She looks at Harry. "Would you like one too?"

He nods. "Yes, ma'am. Thank you."

I peer out the window toward the mobster house. "I wonder if we'll uncover anything new today."

"Doubt it. We'll probably have to entertain ourselves. Daddy and Joe will be looking over and categorizing all those items."

I rest my elbows on the table and drop my chin onto my hands. "Yeah, you're probably right. Now comes the boring part." Harry and I have gotten pretty good over the years at entertaining ourselves while Daddy works.

Mrs. Murphy arrives, carrying a tray that holds two plates and two mugs. After lowering it onto the next table, she reaches for the drinks. "I'll tell you what, I've known all about that house my whole life." She sets the brimming mugs in front of us.

The chocolatey foam looks so enticing, but I wait before indulging myself. I'm curious about what she's going to tell us.

"Is that so?" Harry obviously wants to know more as well.

She nods, glances over her shoulder as if to make sure no one is listening, and then leans close. "Yep. Believe it or not, my mother was a cocktail waitress there at one time."

"Wow!" Scandalous!

She smiles at my excitement. "We have always been a nice law-abiding community, but times were tough, and this little town profited from that 'unique' establishment. The stores, inns, and restaurants all appreciated the extra business provided by the patrons of the speakeasy."

"That makes sense." Harry sips from his mug.

Mrs. Murphy turns to get our breakfast plates. When she sets them in front of us, I stare at the food. Maybe I'm not hungry after all. The scrambled eggs and hash browns are green. At least the bacon looks edible.

She chuckles. "I guess you don't realize what day it is."

I look up at her. "Um . . . Wednesday?"

"It's Saint Patrick's Day. I always make green food to celebrate. Wait until you see the green mashed potatoes I'm serving tonight." She picks up the empty tray and starts to walk away but looks back at us after only a couple of steps. "Did they find the second hidden room yet?"

My gaze goes from her to Harry then back. "Second room?"

She nods. "Sure. There's the large lounge area, of course, but that's not all. The patrons needed a place to hide and a way to escape if the police arrived." With a broad smile she walks away.

Harry and I clink our mugs together. Today may not be as boring as we previously thought.

As soon as we get to the house, Daddy sets us to work. He isn't nearly as excited about finding the second room as we are but promises that when we finish with our work, we can explore.

The large items have already been removed from the crate and taken upstairs, where Joe and his assistants are working. They claimed they preferred working in the natural light. More likely they wanted easier access to the porch for their smoke breaks. Yuck.

That leaves Daddy, Harry, and I in charge of the smaller items, which still need to be catalogued. We don't often get to assist him with his work, so I'm determined to do it perfectly. Since we have the stone basement room to ourselves, we create a little assembly line. I'm assigned to carefully remove items from the giant crate one by one and tag them. Harry then uses our father's 35mm camera to take several photos of each piece. Daddy keeps busy writing down detailed descriptions.

I carefully unwrap a beautiful porcelain doll with a painted face. After tagging it, I hand it to Harry. "What will happen to all of these items?"

"We will attempt to match each of them with the Sultana manifest then try and track down the original owners." Daddy runs his hand along a smooth ceramic vase he is now examining. "Although, I'm guessing from the way the items were haphazardly placed in the crate, there are pieces here that weren't on the Sultana but were treasures Pete DiGiovanni collected over the years." He points to a metal circle in front of him. "For instance, this campaign button is from the William McKinley presidential campaign in the late 1800s, years after the Civil War."

Harry pulls the camera away from his face. "How on earth will the rightful owners ever be tracked down then?"

Daddy finishes jotting something down. "Those items that can't be traced will most likely find homes in various museums."

A small item wedged beneath an old Bible catches my eye. I reach in the crate and pull out a green stone kinda shaped like a shamrock. Different shades of green and brown run through the rough rock like veins. A leather strand loops through a chiseled hole, making the stone a necklace. What a perfect find for Saint Patrick's Day.

An unexpected thud from above makes me jump. Loud voices disturb our peaceful work. Daddy's head turns toward the stone staircase. The raised voices turn to angry shouts.

"I'd better check on that." Daddy lays down his pencil and heads up the steps.

Harry sets the camera aside as we patiently wait for Daddy to return. What could be going on?

A bone-jarring, reverberating blast stops all the shouting.

I gasp.

Harry grabs my arm. "That was a gunshot."

"Daddy." The word barely makes it out of my dry mouth.

"Come on, we've got to hide." My big brother pulls me across the room and behind the massive wooden bar. We cower in the corner, straining to hear any sounds.

Heavy footsteps soon pound down the stairs. Echoing

stomps fill the room. I cower into a tighter ball as icy fear floods through my veins.

"Look at all this loot." The deep voice bears a sharp accent.

"Grab what you want, but you know our orders—we're torching the rest. Everything needs to be destroyed."

I squeeze my hands together and realize I'm still holding the unique necklace. I stroke the stone in an attempt to control my quaking hands. Harry makes the Sign of the Cross, and I force myself to join him in silent prayer.

Dear Lord, please protect us. Blessed Mother Mary, pray for us.

My fingers stroke the curves of the shamrock, reminding me that today is the feast day of Saint Patrick and how he used the shamrock shape in his teachings. *Holy Trinity, help us.*

I take a deep breath, trying to calm myself, but the sharp stench of gasoline terrifies me. They are going to burn this place, with us in it!

Saint Patrick, pray for our safety and a way to escape.

Mrs. Murphy's words from this morning rush into my mind. The patrons of the speakeasy needed a place to hide. Somewhere a second hidden room exists! *But where is it?* I squeeze my eyes shut and picture the room. All the walls are made of rough gray stone. Where could a secret door be located?

My fingers brush the smooth wood of our hiding place. These panels would be excellent camouflage. I crawl along the perimeter of the bar, pushing on the wood. Finally, one moves in a smooth, silent slide, revealing an opening. I yank on Harry's hand and pull him with me.

As we scramble into the space, I notice another stone staircase leading into darkness.

"Good thinking!" Harry whispers as he slides the wooden door shut.

I'm not sure I agree. The complete darkness that now entombs us is almost as terrifying as being in the same room with those thugs. But at least we're safe for the moment.

My forced gratefulness is short-lived as the horrifying scent of smoke sneaks into our hiding place. Panicked, we feel around in the pitch dark and blindly make our way down the stone staircase. I run my hands along the slightly damp stones, letting my imagination run away with me. How many spiders must call this place home? My saddle shoes stick to each step that takes us further down into the unknown. As we go, the muffled sounds from above grow faint, while the stale, dank mustiness increases. The moldy odor of the cellar intermixed with the acrid, smoky fumes turns my stomach. Oh, what I wouldn't give for some clean fresh air! After what feels like an hour, we reach the last step and huddle together in the dark void.

I wipe a tear from my face. "Harry, I'm scared."

He puts his arm around me. "Me, too. Let's pray."

"Oh! Let's ask Saint Patrick to pray for us."

"Um . . ." The doubt in his voice reflects our dire situation.

"It helped last time," I insist. "Right after I asked him to pray for us, I thought of the hidden room. Today is his feast day. Surely if any saint would be able to ask for God's help, it would be the saint of the day."

"I'm not sure that makes any sense, but sure, why not? But we also need to say a Hail Mary and an Our Father."

I rub my thumb along the rough edges of the stone shamrock. "Saint Patrick, please pray for us. We sure could use any extra help and prayers."

I begin to recite the other prayers along with Harry when another thought bombards my mind. "Harry, Mrs. Murphy said the speakeasy patrons used this room so they could escape. That means there has to be an exit!"

"Huh. That makes sense." A spark of hope infiltrates the despair in his voice. "Hold onto my shirt, and we'll feel our way around the room. Maybe we can find another door."

I shove the necklace in my pocket and cling to my brother's shirt. We slowly inch along, running our hands against the rough, clammy stone wall, our feet shuffling along a dirt floor. As we venture further from the house, the sounds of our scuffled footsteps and heavy breathing shift, the timbre closing in around us. Could we now be in some sort of tunnel?

The further we journey into this underground cavern, the cooler the air becomes. I resist the urge to pull my sweater tighter around me, not daring to drop my hand from the wall or relinquish my death-grip on Harry's shirt. Minute after minute slowly creeps past before Harry abruptly stops. My nose smashes into his shoulder. Ouch!

"Why'd you stop moving?" I rub my nose.

"We reached a corner. Oh! It's a staircase."

We crouch down then proceed to crawl up the steps. Peering through the darkness, I can't tell if my eyes are playing tricks or if there is a sliver of light above us. Blinking doesn't make it go away, so the thin yellow strip becomes my beacon of hope.

We finally reach a wooden door.

Harry fumbles around till he finds a knob and twists it. "It's locked."

Aargh! "We can't give up." I bang on the door.

Harry grabs my arm. "What if the bad guys hear us?"

I lean against the exit, blinking back tears. How will we escape? *Oh, Saint Patrick, please keep praying for us.*

Oh! Of course! "Harry! If this was an emergency exit, then there had to be a way to get out. They wouldn't have kept it unlocked because they didn't want just anyone coming in." I run my hands around the icky-damp walls. "Maybe there's a key."

Harry joins in my frantic search. "Another good idea, Grace."

"I think it's Saint Patrick somehow inspiring me."

"Found it!"

For the next few moments, Harry tries to slide the key into the lock. The eventual click is the greatest sound I've ever heard.

Harry shoves on the door with his shoulder, inching it open about half a foot. He grunts, then leans against the wooden portal. "Something must be blocking it."

"I think I can squeeze through." Sometimes it's good to be little. I shimmy my way through the opening. Soon I'm standing in the middle of a forest. The afternoon light filters through overgrown trees and bushes that have practically entombed the long-forgotten exit, which is set into a hill. I yank the vines and branches, and soon we're able to force the door open enough for Harry to escape.

He pushes himself through the narrow opening and wraps his arms around me in a rare display of emotion.

I hug him back then glance around the towering trees that surround us. "Now what? How do we get back to the house?"

Harry bites his lower lip and points over my shoulder. I turn. Billowing smoke pollutes the blue sky above the treetops. Dread grips my heart. *Daddy.* But before we can plan our next move, the welcome sound of screeching sirens permeates the unsettling quiet.

Thank goodness! We exchange a smile then sprint toward the edge of the woods.

Present Day

Luke stares at Grandma, waiting for her to continue, but she smoothly spreads frosting across the cookie in front of her, seemingly content with her story's ending.

"Grandma, what happened next?" Celia sets down her knife, which has remained poised mid-air as she anticipated the finale of the story.

Grandma looks up, surprised. "What?"

"Don't act all innocent." Austin points his half-eaten cookie toward her. "You know that was a lousy place to end the story."

Grandma laughs. "I wasn't sure if I was boring you or not."

Luke loosens his grip on the container of green sprinkles in his hand. Surely there was more to the story. "Did all the items burn?"

"Was your dad hurt?" Celia slips on the oven mitt to rescue the last tray of cookies from the beeping oven.

Austin takes another bite. "Who were those guys? More mobsters?"

"And what did your mom have to say about it all?" The oven door shuts, and Celia sets the hot cookie tray on top of the stove.

"I guess I did leave you hanging just a bit." Grandma removes her glasses and places them on top of her head. They instantly disappear amid her curls. "Well, as it happened, Mrs. Murphy was walking over to the house to deliver a tray of green cupcakes, when the men stormed the home. She ran back to the inn and called the police. Those men were members of the DiGiovanni family. When the news broke that items were found at Eddie the Bull's old speakeasy, they worried that incriminating paperwork about the family's illegal operations would be discovered. They might have slipped away, but in their hurry to leave the area, they sped right past a patrol car and were pulled over. And amazingly, despite some smoke damage, most of the items survived."

She reaches for one of the cooled cookies. "Those thugs had tied up Joe and his associates at gunpoint. Daddy, on the other hand, put up a fight, trying to get back to us, so he was a little roughed up." She laughs. "He was pretty proud of his black eye since it made for a great story to share with his class the next week. Mama, however, was not too happy about our little misadventure. In fact, that was the last time I remember ever staying home alone with Daddy for any extended period of time."

"Wow. I can't believe you never told us about this." Austin licks his fingers.

Celia gives their younger brother a look and points toward the faucet. Austin sighs then slinks over to the sink to wash his hands.

Satisfied, Celia turns back to Grandma. "I agree, how could you not tell us?"

Grandma sifts through the pile of cookie cutters. "It wasn't a story to tell little children. And we stopped getting together on Saint Patrick's Day, so I just never thought about sharing it."

A stab of regret hits Luke for their missed years of cookie-decorating. At least they're here today. "Well, thanks for telling us. So, do you still think Saint Patrick helped you that day?"

Grandma picks up an unfrosted shamrock-shaped cookie. "Yes, I do. You know, saints are our heavenly friends. Not only can they inspire us to be better people, but because they are so close to God, they can intercede on our behalf."

Luke looks down at his hands. Maybe he should ask his confirmation saint to pray for him as he makes his big college decision. Couldn't hurt. Maybe he'd even ask for Saint Patrick's help.

Celia transfers the last of the cookies from the baking sheet to the cooling rack. "What happened to the necklace? Was it sent to a museum?"

"No." Grandma smiles at the shamrock shape in her hand. "That stone shamrock was not on the Sultana's manifest, so they never were able to track down where it had come from. Joe knew how much I liked it so he insisted I keep it."

"Do you still have it?" Austin reaches for another frosted cookie.

Grandma shakes her head. "I kept it for a while, but it didn't feel right to just store it in my jewelry box. Even though the rightful owners couldn't be found, I believed it had some significance since the items in that crate had come from a museum, private collection, or church. Keeping it wasn't the right thing to do. That special stone was meant to be shared with others."

"So, what did you do with it?" Celia settles back on her stool.

Grandma brushes some flour off the back of her hand. "A few months after our ordeal, my father told me about a friend of his whose family was going through a challenging time. After praying about it, I felt sure that Saint Patrick could be of assistance to them as well. So, I encouraged Daddy to send the necklace overseas to his friend."

Austin snaps a frosted rainbow cookie in half and pops a hunk in his mouth. "That's so cool."

"*And...*" A mischievous twinkle shines in Grandma's eyes. "A few years later, we heard that the stone might have actually been a relic of Saint Patrick."

"*Seriously?*" Austin mumbles over his mouthful of cookie.

Luke stares at the shamrock-shaped cookie in front of him. "I wonder how many other people Saint Patrick helped over the years."

Grandma smiles. "I've thought about that over the years. Wouldn't it be incredible to know who else has been blessed because of that beautiful stone?"

Luke nodded. Wouldn't it indeed . . .

Separating fact from fiction: The Sultana was a real ship that sank in the Mississippi River transporting troops home from the Civil War. The DiGiovanni family was a crime family in Kansas City during the 1920s. The author has visited an old speakeasy in a beautiful little town outside of Kansas City. The links between these facts, as written in this story, are purely a result of her imagination.

ABOUT THE AUTHOR

LESLEA WAHL is the author of the award-winning Catholic teen mysteries *The Perfect Blindside, An Unexpected Role, Where You Lead,* and *eXtreme Blindside.* The characters in this short story, Luke, Celia, Austin, and Grandma Grace, appear in her newest adventure novel, *A Summer to Treasure.* Leslea's journey to become an author came through a search for value-based fiction for her own children. She now not only writes for teens but also has become a reviewer of Catholic teen fiction to help other families discover faith-based books. Leslea lives in beautiful Colorado with her husband and children. The furry, four-legged members of her family often make cameo appearances in her novels. Leslea has always loved mysteries and hopes to encourage teens to grow in their faith through these fun adventures. For more information about her faith-filled Young Adult mysteries, please visit www.LesleaWahl.com.

Around the Year 2000,
London, England

7

IN MOUTH OF FRIEND AND STRANGER

by T. M. Gaouette

My head hurt. My heart hurt. My body hurt. Alone and empty, I sat leaning against wrought-iron bars that enclosed a small park in the center of Leicester Square. I released my long hair from my cap, the disguise only necessary at night when pretending to be a boy would be safer.

Leicester Square. Where street musicians hung out, blithely strumming guitars and beating bongo drums. They sat in huddles beside groupies, smoking cigs and supping on cans of Foster's Lager. Instruments told the tale of personal struggle. Passersby stopped and listened, nodding heads in appreciation, smiling at friends or loved ones, and perhaps dropping a few coins into a hat before moving on. Then there were the promising Van Goghs, sitting open-legged on small folding stools outside the Suisse Center, enticing tourists into having their portraits memorialized on edge-wrapped cotton canvas. They flaunted their talents on surrounding easels, chatting with fellow painters in between propositions.

Leicester Square attracted all kinds, some in ripped jeans, others in skirts, suits, or silk gowns. Summer invoked a rainbow of colors, laughter, and screams. The world's cultures drifted through or stopped for a while. People passed on their way to work, back home, or somewhere in between. Kids, old folks, money, rags. Leicester Square offered a world for all appetites within its countless pubs, clubs, wine bars, restaurants, cinemas, and theaters. Leicester Square sat proudly amidst London's Soho, China Town, Covent Garden, and Piccadilly Circus, in the West End of London. And the West End of London was the heart that gave London life.

I could hear the musicians or watch the painters if I wanted to. But I'd heard and seen them all before. I rested my arms on my bent knees, my head hanging casually to one side. I sat still as a statue, ignoring the world around me. The warm breeze of summer flipped my hair across my face. I didn't flinch or try to remove the strands tickling my cheeks, lost in a scene in my mind, the sounds of my surroundings the background music.

It was a painful scene that repeated itself and then transitioned into a similar scene. A scene that will never reveal itself through my lips but will plague my mind forever. I heard again the loud, booming voice of my father, filled with hatred and insults. I saw the contorted face with its glaring stare. I even felt the spit that sprayed from his angry mouth and smelled the beer-scented breath that wafted as he screamed his abuse, but all this was nothing.

As a toddler, the pain had come from a smack on the rear with the sole of a shoe. That was nothing compared to the powerful back-handed slams across the head I received a few years later. That was seven years ago, when I was six. Looking back, those beatings seemed almost harmless. But the seven years since had proved to be the most insane in both our worlds. Now my dad screamed like a madman, and I tried to keep a chair or table between us. He always reached me though. No matter how badly I wanted to run, I couldn't. My legs cemented themselves to the ground and my body shook, and then the worst thing usually happened. No matter how much I tried, no matter how much I held my breath or gritted my teeth, I always started to cry, and that, for me, was suicide.

"So, Hannah's gonna cry, eh? What do I expect from a little girl? You start crying like a typical wimpy female. I told your mum you shoulda been a boy."

I shook my head furiously, wiping tears away with the back of my hand, hoping to erase them before he saw them.

He laughed out loud and shouted, "Too late, little girl!" and he lunged over whatever piece of furniture sat between us. Now I didn't care how much I cried. It was too late anyway.

Brought back to reality by the loud clanging of bells, I gazed around in confusion, quickly wiping tears that streaked my cheeks. The sounds of the bells above the

Suisse Center rang out in loud, piercing chimes. I blinked, recalling my bearings, and noticed a pair of legs standing in front of me, blocking my view. I shifted my glance up to confront the source of the obstruction.

The tramp looked down at me. His gray hair, long and completely matted, blended into a beard that covered most of his face, save for his bent nose and beady eyes. He wore a deep brown suit that hung in rags over his thin body. His left foot was lost in a huge green Wellington boot; his right squeezed itself into a worn-out loafer with holes that ventilated his encrusted toes.

I squinted up at him, still half dazed.

The tramp's beard moved, the butt of a cigarette smoking and bobbing in its midst. I figured he was talking but couldn't see his mouth or hear his voice over the sound of the bells. Not that it mattered. I, like everyone else in London, was familiar with the inquiry, "Can you spare any change?" I shoved a hand into my pocket, pulling out some coins.

The old man waited, his eyes sparkling. After accepting the coins, he cradled them in his palm and poked at them with his finger, counting his spoil before wedging them into his pocket and puffing contentedly.

I couldn't help but smile. It didn't take much to please someone with nothing. Then again, if I kept giving away all my money, I'd end up with nothing, and then what?

The simple clanging of the bells blended into a Suisse melody that I didn't recognize. I gazed up at the clock and watched the small figurines in clogs appear from one side of the clock, travel across its front, and then disappear around the bend. Leaning my head back against the railings, my gaze dropped to an old couple standing arm in arm amongst a crowd of tourists who watched the clock. I rolled my eyes.

"Shut up!" I yelled to the clock. "You're doing my head in." But my voice was drowned out by the continuous sound of the happily chiming bells, and my cut lip, still swollen, stung. I absently watched the little people dance, allowing a tear to trail from the corner of my eye. Every now and then the little people turned and curtsied, and I imagined that they were acknowledging me. I could almost hear their silent words over the dominating chimes. *If you don't shout loud enough, no one will hear you.*

I closed my eyes, wiping my face and rubbing my head furiously, then released a loud sigh. With slow rhythmical movements, I began knocking my head lightly against the railings. Fear grew within me. I must make a decision. Sitting around watching the world go by wasn't helping my situation.

Sucking in another weary sigh, I pushed myself from the ground, the move causing a dull pain in my bruised arm. I looked from left to right, gathered my shoulder-length hair into a twist, and covered my head with the baseball cap. Where now? I grabbed my backpack, carefully swinging it onto my back to avoid further reminders of my father's wrath.

I decided to just walk, drifting through Leicester Square

and toward Covent Garden.

My decision not to return home was a definite one. The abuse I typically experienced would not compare to the punishment I'd receive if my father eventually caught up with me. What additional pain could be inflicted? The risk was worth it. I'd dreamed about running away many times before. Now I'd made my dream come true. And although the reality frightened me, the sentiment of freedom compensated for it.

I had no idea where I was headed, so I allowed my feet to take control, passing shops and restaurants I'd been by many times before, this time without seeing them. Outside the Hippodrome nightclub the crowd thickened as eager clubbers began forming queues at the entrance, with still hours remaining before the club opened. But standing around among friends and fellow ravers made for a great pre-party bash.

I meandered my way through ticket touts bargaining with passersby. A young man in a club t-shirt flitted through the crowd toward me, shoving a leaflet into my chest. I reluctantly grabbed it, then let it fall to the ground, knowing already it was promoting special entrance rates before 10:00 p.m.

The day rolled on and the atmosphere in Leicester Square reflected the anticipation in the minds of everyone. Where some people seemed to have specific destinations, others simply floated along, as if waiting for inspiration.

Crossing the road, I joined a rebellious crowd that paid no heed to the orders of the red man flashing. Head down,

I watched my feet and walked on, looking up on occasion to confirm my direction. I wound my way past slow-walking shoppers and cursed as couples took up the pavement by linking hands. The excitement of Leicester Square was now behind me, and I was glad. I passed shop after shop and finally interrupted my thoughts to look around. I was a block away from Covent Garden, but the idea of facing the commotion of another tourist attraction made me decide instead to traverse the quieter back streets toward Charing Cross.

Charing Cross Station was situated at one end of the Strand. The busy road led its commuters past the Royal Courts of Justice, a number of restaurants, and an array of shops.

"Spare some change?"

The voice came from the entrance of Rhymes Stationery Shop. A boy, dark straggly hair falling over his eyes, sat on a filthy brown blanket, leaning against the glass door. He wore dirty, ripped, faded blue jeans and a worn-out Manchester United t-shirt. He looked older than I, probably around sixteen.

"What are you staring at? Can ya' spare some change or what?"

I quickly reached into my pocket, pulled out some change, and dropped it into his outstretched hand.

"Do you live here?" I said, surprised that the question I was thinking sprang out of my mouth.

"You're a bird," he said, with a grin. "Thought ya' was a bloke." The stranger counted the coins with his grubby hands, reminding me of the tramp earlier.

I responded with a shrug. Why did I even ask the question? The words had just escaped my lips before even registering in my mind. So, I turned to walk away.

"Oi!" The boy rushed after me. "Oi, you!" He gripped my left shoulder and spun me to face him.

A rush of fear flooded through me, and I pulled away.

"Listen, if ya' want, ya' could buy us some grub," the boy said. "And I'll tell ya' me whole life story if you like. I don't care."

"No, it's alright." I was about to turn away again, but the boy grabbed my arm. "Get off me!" I said, shoving the stranger's hand away and trying to sound tough, but my voice cracked and quivered. My throat tightened. *Don't cry, little girl.* But now my fears caused familiar sensations to run through my body. My feet became lead. I wanted to run but my body refused to comply.

"Hey, I ain't gonna hurt ya'." The boy took a step back, as if in an attempt to calm my nerves. "I'm jus' hungry, that's all."

"Well, I ain't got much money," I stammered.

"Ah, come on, luv, jus' a burger 'n fries from ole McD's, I ain't askin' for much, now, am I?"

"Here." I jammed my hand back into my pocket and retrieved a ten-pound note. It was all I had left, but what choice did I have? I held it out to the boy. "Jus' take it, alright? Jus' take it an' leave me alone."

The stranger's eyes darted from my trembling hand to my eyes.

"Take it," I insisted and waved the note in front of his face.

"Listen, luv, I ain't tryna mug ya'." He raised his hands in surrender, his eyes softening. "If I frightened ya', I'm sorry. Keep ya' money."

I lowered my trembling hand.

"M'name's Pat, by the way." The boy feigned a cheerful voice and held out his hand.

I ignored it.

He didn't move. "What a way t'meet, eh?"

I remained silent.

"Okay, I'll jus' talk t'm'self then. Listen, I'm tryna be nice now, alright? I was a bit rough, I admit, but I weren't tryna nick ya' cash, honest. How 'bout I take *you* t'McD's, eh? I think I got enough 'ere to buy us a shake each. What d'ya' reckon?"

The words remained jammed in my throat, fear tightening around them.

"Fine, get lost then." He started to turn away.

"Okay." The assent burst from my lips. I don't really know why, quite honestly.

His response was a wide grin.

Standing in the queue, I offered to buy dinner for Pat after all. I'd felt bad watching him gawk at customers scoffing their meals as we made our way to the counter.

We found a table by the window and Pat unwrapped his Big Mac with slow, precise movements of his fingers, now clean from a quick boys' room detour before ordering. He'd also washed his face and wet his light brown hair, apparently using his fingers to comb the messy strands back off his face to reveal hazel eyes and a strong jaw.

"Mmmmm . . . smell that. I dunno whether to eat it or propose to it." Elbows on the table and leaning in on his food, Pat offered a crooked grin before taking a huge bite.

I neglected my nuggets and fries and sipped my Coke, wondering how I'd survive with the little change that I had left in my pocket.

We sat in silence while Pat shoved as much of his burger into his mouth as possible. In between chews and swallows, he jammed a couple of fries into any vacant space within his cheeks, while taking slurps of his Coke. Every now and then he swiped his nose with his knuckles or glanced around the room, noting the other diners.

I sat quietly watching.

It wasn't long before Pat had devoured his own meal and began eyeing up mine.

"So . . ." He narrowed his eyes at me. "What's ya' name again?"

"Hannah." I wondered if I should have told him another name. Too late now.

He nodded. "Hannah, so, what ya' doing walking the streets a' London all on ya' tod, eh? Can I get a fry?" He reached over and took one of my fries.

I shrugged my response.

He smiled, his eyes sparkling, and slurped the remainder of his drink. "Don't talk much, do ya'?"

With the night drawing on, my thoughts turned to my dad. Likely still at the pub, he probably didn't know I'd even gone anywhere yet. He wouldn't realize till morning, I assumed. "Do you live on the streets?"

"I live wherever I wanna live . . . don't mind if I snag another fry, do ya'?"

I shook my head and waited for Pat to continue.

"It's great, y'know. I do what I want, when I want, and I ain't got no one to tell me jack." He smiled triumphantly. "Plus, I've loadsa' friends who I have a laugh with. I'll tell ya' something for nothing too, the streets are a great place to meet different people. Ya' get all sorts, you'd be surprised . . . May I?" He reached for another fry, shoving it into his mouth before I responded. "Why ya' so interested in the streets? As if I don't already know."

"Well, I was thinking . . . "

"How old are ya'?" Pat interrupted, his forehead crinkling.

"Fifteen," I lied.

He nodded, scratching his chin and smirking as if he could read right through me. "What's wrong with ya' home then? Don't ya' like ya' parents? Have ya' got parents?"

I wasn't sure how much I should tell this stranger. But then again, wasn't I a stranger to him too? So what did it matter? "My mum died when I was little, but my dad's still alive."

He nodded slowly, shifting his glance to the door as a couple entered, then back to me. "So ya' dad gives ya' strife now and then, eh? I heard this one before. Do ya' have any brothers or a sis?"

"No. Anyway, I don't wanna live there anymore."

"Oh, jus' like that? Ya' decided that ya' don't wanna live there jus' like that."

I glared at him. "I got my reasons."

"We all got our reasons, luv . . . you gonna eat that?" Pat pointed to the uneaten meal in front of me.

I cringed. His calling me "luv" was getting annoying. Still, I shook my head and pushed my food across the table. I couldn't eat a bite.

"Ah, sweet, are ya' sure? Thanks, luv. Y'know ya' should really eat something," he advised as he dunked a nugget into a tub of sweet and sour sauce and jammed it into his mouth.

"Can you not call me luv?" I said.

"Wha?" he asked with his mouth full, eyes on me.

"I just don't like it."

He shrugged. "Suit y'self. Anyways, as I was saying," he continued through chews, "we all got our problems, ain't it? But were *yours* worth leavin' the comfort of ya' home?"

"Who said anything about my home being comfortable?" My response was more aggressive than I'd intended. I touched my cut lip with my tongue, my eyes burning with tears and fury, and I dug my nails into my palms.

With all the nuggets eaten, Pat licked his fingers and wiped them on his jeans before settling back in his seat.

His eyes never left mine, and it was making me uncomfortable.

I yanked my cap lower over my face to close him out. My brain was on fire. Here I sat, eating at McDonald's with a total stranger. But something struck me as even odder than that. I figured Pat's interest in my life was purely a polite way of returning the favor of the food, but part of me wanted to tell him the truth about my father. Truth had been wedged inside me for so long, I desperately wanted to let it out. Release it into the world. Lighten my ache. What would Pat do with the truth?

I resented Pat's preaching on the world, and his implication that everyone else's troubles were equal to mine. My left eyebrow throbbed, and I rubbed it with the palm of my hand.

"Ya' really can't go back, can ya'?" Pat's gaze held me, searching mine, his voice serious.

"I think I'd rather die first." A lump formed in my throat.

"Okay, so besides that, what other plans do ya' have?"

I hadn't made other plans. I hadn't had time to think of any. As soon as my dad left for the pub, I'd shoved a bunch of items into my backpack and left the house. Plans were far from my mind. Now I sat in silence.

After too long a pause, Pat cleared his throat and stood up. "Let's get out of 'ere."

Warm air and a dark street greeted us as we stepped outside. The earlier bustle of cars, trucks, bikes, and scooters had died down to an easy stream of passing traffic.

Pat sucked in a lungful of air, followed by a cough and splutter. "Stinkin' pollution," he muttered. "Hannah, I'm gonna be honest with ya'." He nudged my arm as he strutted beside me, both hands shoved in his jeans pockets, eyes glancing all around him. "I lied about the streets, luv." He winced his apology. "They ain't all they're cracked out t'be. Just look around."

I followed his nod. As the evening introduced itself, the storeowners closed the doors behind their last customers, and the true residents of the Strand took their regular places in front of their chosen retailer, setting up their homes for the night. Every age, men and women, scattered along the pavement. Where had they all come from? Some carried dirty old blankets, others newly found cardboard boxes. Some looked to be my age, a fact that did not comfort me.

We passed one shop entrance housing a group of laughing young men. One of them begging for money. The next sheltered a solitary old man huddled in his box, then in the next, someone hidden under a blanket with only eyes showing. Dead eyes, sad eyes, lonely eyes, hungry eyes. I saw all these eyes as Pat and I walked on, recording them amongst the other horrors that plagued my thoughts.

"For every day that I'm happy, I suffer at least another five days of a complete nightmare," Pat continued. "Everyone does. Teens who run away are looking for better days. Course, a few run jus' coz it looks good or coz their dad won't buy 'em a BMW, but that don't last long. Others run for real reasons." He paused before we crossed a road, picking up speed as the lights changed and cars headed our way.

Pat stole a look at me. "They run from messed up parents or foster homes, but it ain't right. This place's flooded with perverts and murderers." He scratched the back of his head during this next short pause, tossing a glance over his shoulder. "M'point is . . . if ya' wanna be safe, ya' better know where ya' running to and ya' better get there fast. The streets ain't a place for no one, let alone a young girl like you. Know what I'm saying?"

I nodded.

"Case in point . . ." he muttered, his pace slowing.

"What?" I looked at him, following his stare to two guys watching us from a shop doorway across the road.

Pat quickened his pace again and I followed suit. The men trudged toward us.

"Run," Pat whispered and grabbed my hand, yanking me down a side street and pulling me into a sprint. My backpack bounced on my bruised back as we ran. His grip tightened around my fingers, leaving me no choice but to run wherever he guided me. Up one road, down another, and always those two men were behind us, catching up as I slowed down, my chest burning.

Back on a main street, Pat dragged me into the entrance of Charing Cross Road Station, the men hot on our heels. He released my hand and jumped over the gate, then waited while I clambered awkwardly over it. No one was there to see us, thank goodness. We ran down a moving escalator so fast I thought I'd fall on my face. Then, just as we entered a platform, a train sat waiting. Pat grabbed my arm and together we jumped on just as the doors closed behind us. We turned, panting, seeing the guys stuck on the platform, faces red with fury, one pointing at Pat with a threatening forefinger.

We sat breathless in the seats of a mostly empty carriage, and I wondered whom I'd taken up with. Was Pat a criminal?

"That was close." He dragged the fingers of both hands through his hair, leaning back in his seat and stretching out his legs.

I looked at him.

"Consequences of livin' on the streets," was all he had to offer with a crooked grin.

I took his word, fearful now that I'd made a huge mistake.

"Sorry," Pat said.

I looked at him, not sure what to say. Maybe I should get off at the next stop and be on my way alone.

"But this is what I was on about earlier. The streets ain't a place for ya'."

"Not sure I got much choice though," I mumbled.

"Ya' got any other family?" he said, getting back to my business.

"I got my grandparents, my mum's parents, that is, but I ain't seen 'em since she died. Plus, my dad hates 'em something chronic. He says they're Bible thumpers, whatever that means."

He stroked his chin. "D'ya' think they'd help ya'?"

"They probably forgot all about me."

"I doubt it. Do ya' know where they live?"

"No, but I know their names from a photo album. Used to be my mum's. And I know they work at a museum. At least, they did back then."

"Well, that's a start."

I sighed, shaking my head. "Pat, who's about to take in a total stranger?"

"Forget that, mate. They're ya' grandparents."

"Yeah, but they ain't never kept in touch with us."

"Oh, and ya' think ya' dad didn't have nothin' to do with that? What are their names?"

"Simon and Beatrice Patterson."

The train stopped again, and the doors slid open. "Come on." Pat grabbed my hand and yanked me out of my seat and off the train.

I stood against a wall next to the ticket machine, eyeing the small grouping of passengers lost in their own business. But for the random bursts of passengers appearing from rising escalators to my right, freed from tube arrivals and scurrying toward exits, the station was quiet this time of night. Every now and then a voice echoed from the Tannoy speakers to inform Tottenham Court Road passengers of delays or cancellations.

The few passengers new to the underground protocol craned their necks, trying in vain to understand the indistinguishable jaded words. Tube veterans, in contrast, continued on their journey without concern, their knowledge likely resting upon the fact that Tannoy messages are habitually erroneous. I absently balanced a ten-pence piece on my right thumb knuckle.

"Okay, so I have seven Simon Pattersons." Pat approached with a torn-out page from a telephone directory. "There any way ya' could narrow it down?"

"I don't know. Maybe. "

"Well, ya' have any idea where they live?" He looked at the page. "I got . . . Seven Sisters, Mile End, Chelsea, the Isle a' Dogs, Enfield, Ealing Broadway—"

"Ealing Broadway," I repeated.

His eyes shot up to meet mine, bright with anticipation. "Is that it?"

"I dunno," I shrugged. "But it sounds familiar." It did, but for the life of me, I didn't know why.

"They all sound familiar, luv." He narrowed his eyes and gritted his teeth. "Sorry."

"Yeah, but I have a feeling, don't I?"

"Great, ya' gonna call this one coz y'got a *feeling*."

"Hey, I ain't callin' no one. It was *your* idea."

Pat raised his hands. "Forget that, they're *your* grandparents."

"Well, I ain't gonna call them. I dunno what to say."

Pat sighed, dragging his fingers through his hair. "Fine, I'll do it. I ain't got nought t'lose, right?"

We meandered our way around a small gathering of passengers to the phone booth.

"Alright then, so what's ya' surname then? And what's y'mum 'n dad's name?"

"Patricia and Larry Bissett."

I watched my new friend's finger circle the dial but wanted to reach out and stop it. Still, I didn't.

Pat said he had nothing to lose, and so I decided that the same went for me, although that internal declaration failed to suppress a nervous sensation that crept up my chest. It expanded as I considered the reality and possible consequence of this one phone call. What if they denied me? What if they called my dad? What if they really had forgotten me?

"'Ello?" Pat's voice broke into my thoughts, and my heart leaped into my throat.

"'Ello, is this Mrs. Beatrice Patterson? . . . oh, hi! . . ." He signaled a thumbs up sign as I pressed my nails into my palms and chomped on my bottom lip. "Ya' don' know me, but I'm a friend a Hannah Bissett, daughter of—" He shot a glance at me, eyes wide in question.

I mouthed my parents' names.

"Oh, yeah! Daughter of Patricia 'n Larry Bissett . . . y'know who I'm on about? . . . m'name's Pat . . . no, I'm a fr . . . well, I'm talking about Hannah . . . see, she's havin' a bit a'bother at home from 'er 'ole man and she's left home and . . ."

I shoved Pat's shoulder, not sure he should disclose my personal details prematurely.

Pat responded with a shrug and a scowl. "No, miss, I ain't playing games . . . hold on, you talk to 'er." With that,

Pat shoved the phone into my reluctant hand.

I stood open-mouthed.

"Go on." Pat smiled cheekily. "Speak to ya' nan."

I lifted the heavy receiver. It smelled like bad breath and cigarettes. I dared not look at the mouthpiece, holding it away from my ear enough so that I could still hear.

"Hello?"

"Okay, now I think that you children have had enough fun for one night." The female voice didn't sound recognizable at all. I didn't know why it would, but I did detect a slight tremble in the woman's voice and cursed myself for agreeing to go ahead with this.

"I'm really sorry," I said, turning away from Pat for privacy and attempting to articulate my words. "I jus' wanted to call you because I have no one else."

"Hannah, if this is really you, then would you mind telling me why you're calling at such a late hour?"

"Actually, I really didn't know how late it was. I'm sorry."

Pat walked around me, his eyes staring at me, as if guessing the full conversation from what he heard on my end.

"Where are you calling from?"

"We're in Tottenham Court Road Station."

"Who are you with?"

"A friend. I met him tonight. His name's Pat." I caught Pat's eye now, as he offered an exaggerated grin. I rolled my eyes, trying not to smile, and looked away. "He lives on the streets." I was aware that I was rambling but didn't try to control it. Instead I tried to comprehend the fact that I was conversing with my grandmother. I listened to her soft, firm voice, and the way that she questioned me made me smile. She didn't really know me, but she seemed to care.

"Hannah, do you think you should be associating with strangers in the middle of the night? Where is your father?"

"Pat already told you that I ran away from home."

"Well, I suppose you are at that stage, aren't you? How old are you now?"

I turned from Pat again and whispered, "Thirteen."

"I don't think it's a very good idea for you to be gallivanting around the streets in the middle of the night, Hannah, especially with a strange boy. Anything could happen." There was a pause and I wondered if she'd put the phone down. But then she added, "Maybe you should sort things out with your father and go home?" The tide turned. I couldn't believe what I'd heard. She didn't care at all. I squeezed my burning eyes shut.

"Actually, I'm not going home," I said stubbornly. "I already decided that." I opened my eyes, finding Pat standing in front of me again, watching with a concerned stare. "I was calling to see if you could help me." There was another slight pause as I waited for her reaction.

Pat scrunched his brows, lifting his hands in question, mouthing, "What?"

I turned from his inquiring stare. "Listen," I said. "I think that maybe this was a bad idea. I'm sorry to have bothered you." Anger swelled in me, heating my cheeks, and I kicked the wall. "I'm gonna go now." I rubbed my eyebrow aggressively and was about to replace the receiver onto its cradle when I heard her clear her throat.

"Hannah? . . . Hannah, I must admit that I'm having a very hard time registering this conversation . . . I haven't seen or heard about you in years. I also feel pressured into making some drastic decision that could end up with us both in a lot of trouble. Your father's not going to be happy one bit, if he cares at all." She muttered the last few words, then she sighed heavily. "Okay, Hannah, you can come and stay with us tonight. I'm not promising anything more. Besides, I'd feel more comfortable if we spoke face to face. Do you know how to get to Ealing Broadway Station?"

"Yes."

"Fine. I will meet you there in twenty minutes."

"Okay."

I hung up the phone and turned to Pat, whose wide eyes and questioning grin beckoned a full and descriptive summary of the conversation.

"I have to meet her in twenty minutes."

"There ya' go!" Pat's face beamed. "I told ya' it would all work out."

But I was not so enthusiastic. The truth rang in the old woman's heavy sighs and long pauses. "No, she really doesn't care. She'll let me stay tonight, but she doesn't sound too happy about it."

"Yeah, but she'll have t'help ya'," he said, squeezing my

shoulder. "She's ya' nan."

"She don't have to do nothing, Pat." I pushed my way past him, heading to the ticket machine. He rushed to keep up.

"Come on, ya' jus' have to be more positive, that's all." He stood facing me, blocking my access to the ticket machine. "Listen, Hannah. Ya' go 'n meet with her tonight, and if things don't work out, then ya' come back 'n find me. I'm always around. Jus' ask for Pat." He held my gaze a few seconds before smiling sincerely, and then he turned and began walking away.

"Wait!" I punched the grubby buttons for my ticket, grabbing it as it appeared in the hatch below.

Pat continued walking. "Gotta go!" He raised his hand in another wave but didn't look back.

"Thanks!" I shouted after him, and my voice echoed around me.

"No problem!" he yelled as he climbed the steps that led into the night.

"I'll see ya' tomorrow!" I shouted the words, but there was no response.

I stood on the escalator, watching the ground rise to me. My steps slowed as I made my way through the tunnels toward the platform.

Other than a young couple at the far end of the platform, I was alone. Again. I sat on a wooden bench and glanced up at the message board that informed me that my train would be arriving in three minutes. Three minutes and then what?

I leaned back and closed my eyes. Pat's smiling face appeared in my mind.

I had no idea what awaited me at the end of my journey, but I wondered if it would include my new friend. He said I could come back and look for him if things didn't work out. But maybe if they did work out, I could still look for him.

The tube faintly rumbled in the black arch of the tunnel. I stood and walked to the edge of the platform. Looking down, I watched as two little mice scuttled between the tracks and disappeared beneath me.

The rumbling got louder, and I stared into the darkness, watching as the two bright lights appeared from the abyss and slowly grew larger. Soon I saw the shape of the tube as it raced toward me and finally exploded through the hole. I stayed by the platform's edge, feeling the force of the air as it tried to blow me off balance. The train became a blur as it rushed past my eyes. Then it screeched to a halt. The doors slid open lazily in front of me, as if welcoming me into a new world. This could be it. I stepped into the empty carriage and took a seat to my left, dropping my backpack to the floor between my legs. A whole new future. A whole new life.

"So, I was thinking." A voice broke into my thoughts. I looked up to see Pat standing beside me in the doorway just as the doors closed abruptly behind him and the train sluggishly started moving ahead.

"What are you doing here?" I said.

"Well," he began, moving around me and taking the seat to my left. "I ain't much of a gentleman if I let ya' travel on the tube alone in the middle of the night, am I now?"

I shrugged, happiness filling me at having my new friend with me.

A few people came and went as we sat side by side, staring out the window and watching darkness and lighted platforms whiz by.

Pat leaned back against his seat, searching his jean pocket now, and pulled out something. It looked like a splotchy flat rock, maybe about an inch wide. Circular in shape, but with uneven edging.

He saw me watching. "From me mum," he said.

"What happened to her?"

"Dead," he said, eyes on the rock. "Me dad too, right before I was born. Me mum when I was small." He closed the rock in a fist and shut his eyes, resting his head back against the glass of the window. "I don' remember much about 'er, but I can hear 'er voice whispering . . ."

Pat paused before speaking in soft, measured words. "'Christ be within me, Christ behind me, Christ before me, Christ beside me, Christ to win me, Christ to comfort and restore me, Christ beneath me, Christ above me, Christ in quiet, Christ in danger, Christ in hearts of all that love me, Christ in mouth of friend and stranger.'"

I noticed a single tear fall down his cheek.

"Christ," I repeated softly, finding comfort in the name.

"Yeah." Pat lifted his head, opened his eyes, and quickly swiped the tear away with the back of his fist that still enclosed the rock. "Jesus Christ. She said He lived on earth thousands a' years ago and was actually God's Son." He looked at me as if waiting for a reaction.

I had none to give.

"Apparently, God, His Son, and their Spirit surround us, all the time." He gestured with his hands. "And they're all one, like a shamrock. I guess some saint called Patrick explained it that way."

"A shamrock?"

"I dunno." He shrugged, a soft smile on his lips. "It's a leaf or something with three parts. Kinda like the shape of this rock, see?" He opened the hand holding the marble-looking rock in his palm. Then he flipped it a few times, revealing the varying shades of green and brown, from a deep dark to a lighter hue, swirling into each other. It looked a bit like a clover leaf, now that he mentioned it, although rough around the edges.

"Mum gave it to me the night she died," he said in a quiet voice. "Pushed it into me palm 'n closed me fingers around it, like I should never let it go. Said a friend sent it to 'er after me dad died. Said she needed it. Whatever that means. She said that's why she named me Patrick." He smiled at me. "She told a story about 'im, but I don't remember much of it. Wish I did, now." He looked back at the rock. "But I'm f'getting so much."

I didn't know anything about any Patrick. And although I had heard the name Jesus Christ, I didn't know much about Him either. Still, my heart ached for Pat. I wasn't sure who had the worst story.

Pat sniffed and looked up as the train stopped at the next station. He sat up straight, sucking in a breath before blowing it out loudly.

"Anyways, whoever Saint Patrick is, I remember them words. And at night, when I'm . . ." He stopped, looking at me as if reluctant to proceed. But then he added, "scared . . ." He swallowed hard. "I say 'em, and it helps. 'Coz I think of me mum, and that saint, and how they believed that this *Christ* watched over 'em like in that poem." He stared at the rock. "Maybe He's watching over me too. Protecting me. Maybe all three of 'em." He looked up at me now. "Sounds daft, eh?" He offered an embarrassed smile.

"No," I said. "No, it sounds real nice."

"Except, last part don't make sense." Pat laughed softly, flicking the rock so it spun in the air, and then caught it. "Christ in mouth of friend and stranger?" He shook his head. "Sounds a bit cannibalistic if ya' ask me."

Christ in mouth of friend and stranger. I thought about the words too. They were strange. We sat silent again, and my attention shifted to where we were. I'd have to pay attention when we came into the next station. So, I watched the blackness until it faded into nothing.

It felt like only a moment later when a lurch of the tube woke me, and I found myself leaning my head on Pat's shoulder. I straightened.

"Sorry," I said, my cheeks warming.

He grinned wide. "No worries. You was out cold."

"Where are we?" I tried to crush a yawn and glanced at the map.

"Headin' into 'olland Park," he said looking up at the map with me. "Ya' can sleep some more."

"No, I'm good." I noticed his hand resting on his knee, holding that rock again, flat on his palm. He rubbed it with his thumb.

"Sorry ya' dad hurt ya'," he said.

A lump rose in my throat. He'd said it with such a soft voice, I was almost sure he actually cared.

His eyes glistened. "And, sorry ya' didn't get t'know ya' mum. Never got any memories of 'er." There was a definite crack in his voice.

"Sorry you lost your mum 'n dad," I said.

"We're a pair, ain't we?" He grinned again, but this time I saw sadness in his eyes.

I looked at the rock in his hand again and took it from him. It was warm in my hand as I held it palm up on my knee. We must have sat staring at it for ages, but then he placed his hand flat on mine, palm down on top of the rock. I dropped my head to his shoulder again, a tear falling down my cheek, and he intertwined his fingers with mine.

What a pair we were.

Ealing Broadway came too fast for my liking and we walked the quiet platform, up the stairs, and into the dark night without one word.

Outside the darkness and warmth wrapped around me. I peered around, nerves filling my stomach as I looked for the grandmother whom I'd never met.

"What if she don't show?" I said.

"She will," he said.

I searched the darkness from one end of the street to the other.

"Ya' nan," Pat said. "Ya' said she was a Bible thumper."

I turned to him. "My dad said it."

He leaned a shoulder against the wall, scratching his arm and crossing his ankles. "Well, then maybe she knows the story of Saint Pat. The one me mum told me."

"Maybe."

He paused, searching the street with a swift gaze before adding, "If she does, will ya' come find me 'n tell me it?"

My cheeks flushed and warmth washed through me. "Yeah, of course."

He looked at me now. "Ya' promise?"

"I promise."

He grinned wide now.

"Hannah?" A voice called out to me. Ahead by the street, a figure stood by a car, just a silhouette in the darkness. It slowly approached.

Pat pushed himself off the wall and stepped away from me. "Well, see, there ya' go. I'll be off then."

"What?" I looked from him to my nan.

"She's 'ere. Ya' good, right?" He tried to smile, but that

sadness was still there, settled in his hazel eyes.

"Hannah, is that you?" the woman said, getting closer.

"Don't leave yet," I said. Almost begged. They were both strangers, but Pat had become my friend. I trusted him.

"Ah, it's getting late, luv, I gotta get back my way 'fore someone steals me spot." Then he closed his eyes tight and gritted his teeth. "I'm sorry. Bad habit."

I smiled, feeling my cheeks warm. "It's alright. I kinda like it now."

He grinned but then just stood, waiting, as if not wanting to go as much as I didn't want him to. "Don't forget to get the scoop on that Saint Pat geezer," he added, attempting to sound cheerful.

"I won't forget," I said. "And then I'll find you."

"Ya' know where t'find me." He was about to turn away.

"Wait," I said. And I rushed to him, wanting to hug him or something, but once I reached him, I just stood there. Feeling awkward. I wanted to hug him. It felt right.

"Come 'ere," he said, wrapping his arms around me. "It'll be good, you'll see. Everything'll work out nice for ya'."

"What about you?"

"Ahh, don't worry about me. No matter what, I ain't alone." He gave me one last squeeze.

"Christ be within you, Patrick."

He laughed. "Yeah, Christ be within ya', Hannah," he said.

And then he let me go. He smiled a warm, 'it's gonna be great' smile, before removing my cap. My hair dropped to my shoulders. "There she is," he said softly. "Ya' safe now." He handed me my cap, then turned and walked back toward the station.

"I'll find you, y'know," I called out.

He turned back to me, walking backward as he smiled wide. "I 'ope so, Hannah."

Then behind me, my nan called, "Hannah."

I turned to face my grandmother.

On the drive to my grandmother's house with another stranger I'd have to get to know, I gazed out into the darkness, tears welling in my eyes.

"Was that the stranger you met tonight?" my nan said.

"He's my friend now," I said. *Friend and stranger.*

Opening my fist, I looked at the rock lying in my palm. When we had reached Ealing Broadway, Pat had let my hand go, but he'd left the rock in my palm. I'd held it in my fist until now and almost forgot it was there.

"Ooh, what's that?" She glanced at the rock while still keeping an eye on the road.

"He gave it to me." I held it up for her to see. "It's a rock."

She looked at it with expert eyes. "Ahh . . . a gift from a friend is a treasure."

"You think?"

"I have an eye for treasure," she said kindly. "It looks like a shamrock?"

I smiled. "Yeah, you know about shamrocks?"

"Well, I'm not a shamrock connoisseur or anything," she said with a short laugh.

My smile melted. I didn't know what that meant, so I peered back out the window.

"Although, I *do* happen to know a story about a man named Patrick and a shamrock . . . if you're ever interested in hearing it."

Often, Christ comes to us in the most unlikely way and at the most unusual time, but always when He's much needed. We see this in "In Mouth of Friend and Stranger." Christ comes in the words of a stranger delivered through a Saint's vestige. Words that remind both characters that they're never alone. This element of discovery is characteristic of T. M. Gaouette's fiction and inspires a desire to think a little more deeply when it comes to knowing, loving, and serving God. For more stories with exciting twists and colorful characters, reflecting God's mercy, check out her Faith & Kung Fu Series.

ABOUT THE AUTHOR

T.M GAOUETTE is the author of the Faith & Kung Fu series for young adults, as well as *The Destiny of Sunshine Ranch* and *For Eden's Sake*. She also contributed to the last two Catholic Teen Books anthologies, *Secrets: Visible & Invisible* with her short story "Sister Francesca" and *Gifts: Visible & Invisible* with "Just Jesus." Her novels have received the Catholic Writers Guild Seal of Approval. *For Eden's Sake* also received an endorsement from Evangelist Alveda C. King in addition to winning a first place Catholic Press Association award.

Born in Africa, raised in London, England, Gaouette now lives on a small farm in New England with her husband, where she homeschools their four children, raises goats, and writes fiction for teens and young adults. A former contributor for *Project Inspired*, Gaouette's desire is to instill the love of God into the hearts of her readers. You can find out more at www.TMGaouette.com.

In the Future, England

THE UNDERAPPRECIATED VIRTUES OF GREEN-FINGERED MONSTERS

by Corinna Turner

KYLE

Pain.

The worst headache ever. Waves of throbbing agony from both sides of my forehead, meeting in a pulsing epicenter in the middle of my brain. Ow.

I didn't dare move in case it made it worse.

Gradually I grew sufficiently used to the pain to become aware of what I could hear and smell. Beeping. Brisk footsteps passing to and fro. Voices murmuring here and there, some slurred, some louder and more business-like. A strong smell of cleaning products and . . . and . . .

Uh-oh . . .

Gingerly, I coaxed my eyelids open. *Ow.* Too bright.

I tried again, inching them up slowly.

Yep. Pale blue walls. Tubular metal bed. IV line in my

wrist. Hospital. The last place a Believer like me wanted to be. How did I get here? I didn't remember being hurt. I didn't remember anything since . . . um . . . I came home from school, right? When was that?

"Ah, you're awake." Brisk but smiling, a nurse appeared by the bed with a tray holding a cup and a little pill pot. "How do you feel?"

"Uh . . . my head hurts a bit."

"Yes, I imagine it would. You have a concussion."

Concussion? Despite my slow, fuzzy thoughts, relief filled me. That wasn't something they could cure by sticking a stolen organ inside me. Because if I refused one . . . they'd take me—or wheel me, the way I felt right now—straight before a judge to make the Divine Denial. And if I refused to make that . . .

"Here."

I accepted the pills eagerly. Bog standard painkillers, from the nasty taste. Usually I tried to offer up little things like headaches for the agonizing discernment of my vocation, but my head was splitting. And I could hardly refuse, here and now. Far too odd—and therefore suspicious.

The nurse watched me taking the pills—checking my motor control? My hand shook slightly, but everything seemed to be working okay. Soon she pulled a networkAccessor from her pocket. "Now, what's your name?"

"Kyle. Kyle Verrall."

She typed that on the screen, nodded, and smiled. "And

how old are you, Kyle?"

"Uh . . . sixteen."

More nodding and smiling. "And where do you live?"

She wasn't writing anything more down . . . oh, she'd found my ID entry and she was just checking that *I* still knew this stuff.

My stomach gnawed at me, emptily, when I woke up again. Fortunately a lunch trolley soon came around and a bored-looking young man put a meal in front of me. I'd almost finished—chewing carefully to avoid moving too suddenly—when the smiley nurse arrived with more pills.

"How are you feeling?"

"Better. My head doesn't hurt as much. What happened to me?"

"You don't remember?"

I almost shook my head, then thought better of it and said, "Not very well," instead.

"Took a tumble off your bike, according to the"—her lips tightened in a disdainful expression—"to the man who brought you in. He was driving along Marlpeak Road behind you and saw you hit a pothole. You went over the handlebars into a tree, then hit the tarmac. That's why you've got two eggs on your head." She tutted sympathetically.

"Can I call my mum and dad?"

"We already contacted them. They'll be along in a bit with some overnight things."

"Overnight?"

"The doctor said you'll have to stay several days, remember?"

"Oh." Doctor? Yes, she'd come in before I fell asleep. "Right. I wasn't concentrating well, earlier."

"No, poor dear. You're going to have to take it easy for quite a while." She looked at my swollen forehead again, tutted some more, shook her head, and bustled off.

I tried to relax and wait for the pills to kick in. My head did feel *better*, it wasn't a lie, but that wasn't the same as it feeling *good*.

I tried to remember the crash, but I couldn't call to mind any memory of cycling anywhere recently, let alone falling off. And something about the whole bicycle business jarred my thoughts, like a discordant note. Why?

Despite that, I was drowsing when a nurse's voice nearby caught my attention. "Here he is. You can't stay long, though. He's got a bad concussion . . . "

Mum and Dad? I sat up eagerly, wincing as renewed pain stabbed through my head—then my eyes fell on the man entering the room and my happy anticipation shattered.

A crisp dark blue uniform with yellow piping.

A detective.

My heart rate kicked up. I winced again, putting one hand to my forehead and shifting slightly in the bed as though trying to get comfortable, seeking to camouflage my dismay.

Remember, I could hear Uncle Peter saying, *all pursuivants are detectives, but not all detectives are pursuivants. Always assume they're not a priest-catcher, stay calm, and act natural. They may have no interest in breaches of the religious suppression laws at all.*

But . . . but . . . had Mum and Dad been arrested?

No. Stop it, Kyle. Mum and Dad and Uncle Peter trained you better than this. Assume he's not a pursuivant and act natural, idiot!

A scrape and a clatter drew my attention back to the man as he deposited a chair beside my bed. He sat down, placing a networkAccessor on his lap, then glanced at me.

"Ah, you're awake. Kyle Verrall?"

"Yes." I eyed his uniform and widened my eyes eagerly. "Hey, are you a detective?" One could be curious and excited with the police, perhaps a touch nervous, but should never, ever come across as really scared. That suggested something to hide. So I'd had it drilled into me since I was old enough to recognize a copper at all.

Were Mum and Dad okay? Were they even now being led before a judge and ordered to make the Divine Denial? *Stop it, Kyle!*

"Yes, I am." He flicked his insignia with one finger. "I'm Sergeant-Inspector Renkin. I'm just here to follow up on the little accident you had yesterday morning."

Yesterday? Ugh, Mum and Dad and Margo must've been freaking out!

I smiled obligingly at him. Sergeant-Inspector wasn't a high rank. That was reassuring.

"Can you tell me what happened?"

"Of course." I reached for the glass of water on the

bedside table and took a sip to give myself thinking time. Was this normal? The nurse hadn't implied there was anything suspicious about my accident. Boys fell off their bikes every day, right? So why was he here? Did they think a car might've hit me? Or was there something else going on that I couldn't remember? A soft whisper in my gut that might've been the Holy Spirit or just my own intuition urged caution.

"To be honest, my memories are pretty upside down." That was true. And for the rest, I'd tell him the only "truth" I had available to me. "But I was cycling along Marlpeak Road—out in the Fellest, y'know—and I hit a bad pothole and came off. The guy who brought me to the hospital said I managed to hit a tree *and* the road, that's why I'm so lumpy!" Proudly, I turned my head to show off both bumps.

A hint of a smile crossed the detective's face. "Yes, very impressive. Well, that all checks out. I'm glad you're on the mend."

Was that it? Was he going to leave?

No . . . He switched on the networkAccessor. "Just one other thing. Have you ever seen this before?"

He placed the accessor in my lap. I peered at the screen, which showed a photograph of a small stone . . . pendant? Three circular leaves curved out from a short stem. Beautifully carved in greenish-brown stone, it looked quite lifelike.

And familiar.

The whisper in my gut grew louder, as though the

ghosts of lost memories screamed a warning.

Two days earlier . . .

MARGO

"Look!" Leaping up from the sofa and crossing to where Bane and I were wiling away the wet Friday evening building a card castle, Kyle slapped a newspaper down beside us so hard that our edifice collapsed in the draft.

"Hey!" objected Bane. "This had better be good!"

Kyle pointed to the headline. "*Look.* Someone's stolen Saint Patrick's Shamrock from the museum. Or I suppose I should say 'Ancient Irish Artifact No. 36.'"

"So?" said Bane. "I'd have thought you'd be pleased, seeing that the EuroGov were fixing to destroy it after that stupid academic outed it as an item of religious significance."

"Well, it depends who took it, doesn't it?" said Kyle.

I pulled the paper towards me, scanning the text. "They're blaming the Resistance? Seriously? What would the Resistance want with a relic?"

I was kind of speaking to Bane, since he'd been hanging out with members of the Young Resistance for months, alas.

"Nothing that I can think of," said Kyle. "It's weird."

"I dunno, maybe they're just trying to give the EuroGov a red face," Bane said, though it was clear from his tone that he was speculating, not in-the-know on this. "It's not like the museum is well guarded. Humiliate the EuroGov for next to no risk."

"Huh, there we go, Kyle," I said.

Another frown crossed my big brother's face, though. "But what are they going to do with it? Now they've got it? It's nothing to them."

"Wrong," said Bane. "It is something to them, because it's something to the EuroGov. If they destroyed it, they'd be doing the EuroGov's work for them. They won't want to hold onto it, though—that little rock will be hot stuff."

The doorbell rang before I could reply. Who was calling at this time? Bane and Kyle were now having a tug of war over the newspaper, Mum and Dad were away on their special anniversary weekend, and Father Mark was in the spare room, so I headed into the hall, shouting, "I'm getting it," up the stairs. After a glance through the peephole, I unlocked the door at once, letting in a middle-aged man before shutting the door quickly behind him to keep the weather out.

"Uncle Peter, what are you doing here?" Father Mark was staying with us at the moment and, except for special feast days, both priests took care never to be in the same place in case of a raid by pursuivants.

"Mark said he needed to speak to me urgently." Uncle Peter slipped off a sodden anorak and hung it on a hook in the hall.

He squelched straight upstairs to find Father Mark, so Bane and I went back to our construction efforts since Kyle had retreated to his room to brood over the newspaper.

KYLE

Sitting down on my bed, I started to read the article again—then sighed and tossed the newspaper aside. What was the point? If the Resistance did have the shamrock, I couldn't do a thing about it. And better than the EuroGov destroying it, right?

As I headed towards the stairs, a murmur of voices came from the guest room. I meant to walk straight past but caught the words "Saint Patrick's Shamrock" and found myself with my ear to the hinge.

"And the message said . . . ?" Uncle Peter's voice.

"Two AM, under Caella Crag, and they'll give it to me."

What? The Resistance were going to give the Shamrock to us, to the Underground?

"Do you believe it?"

"Well, I believe they've got it," Father Mark replied. "What do you want me to do? It's your decision."

Just think . . . the Shamrock of Saint Patrick!

A rustle behind me caused me to spin around, my cheeks heating, but it was Margo and Bane, of course. Mum and Dad were away. Their first overnight holiday in, like, ever, so it was easy to forget.

Eyes narrowed with curiosity, Margo and Bane both joined me outside the door at once so, guiltily, I carried on listening.

"If we could trust them," Uncle Peter was saying, "I'd say go and get it. It's an incredibly special relic of Saint Patrick. A real treasure of the ages." *That was certainly true. A rare survivor—so many relics had been destroyed by the*

EuroGov. "So, *do* you trust them?"

Father Mark laughed bleakly. "No. Not for one single second."

"Then you don't go."

What? I saw my dismay mirrored on Margo's face.

"Are you sure?" Father Mark sounded conflicted.

"Yes, I'm sure." Uncle Peter's voice was firm. "Think about it, Mark. Only three out of five young men make it to the Vatican alive to test their vocation to the priesthood. And only seven out of ten of those who make it through the intensive training safely reach their parish and make it through their first year of ministry, as you are well on track to do. Underground priests—and sisters—are formed in blood, sweat, and tears and are the greatest treasures we have. If there's any doubt—then you don't go. It's not even a hard decision, Mark."

"No, I see that. Tantalizing, though. I'd only need to show up and we'd have the Shamrock of Saint Patrick, safe. Think what that would do for morale."

"You answered the only question that mattered, so the answer is still no." Judging by Uncle Peter's steely tone, he was unmoved—or determined to be.

I caught a faint noise that might've been a sigh from Father Mark. I knew how he felt. My heart had sunk to my trainers. Uncle Peter really wouldn't let him go?

The phone rang downstairs. Bane didn't move, but Margo shot me an alarmed look. Oh yeah, if none of us answered it . . .

I darted quietly down the stairs and grabbed the

receiver.

"Hello?"

No answer. Sales call. I wanted to rush back upstairs and carry on listening, but . . . I was ashamed I'd eavesdropped. I just hadn't been able to help myself. Hmm. In my head I could already hear Uncle Peter saying, "Yes, you could've, Kyle, if you'd really wanted." So I'd have to take it to confession.

To one of them. Oh joy.

Turning my back on the stairs, I went into the living room.

MARGO

"Do you really think they were just going to hand it over?" asked Uncle Peter, though not in a tone that suggested he'd changed his mind.

"I don't know," said Father Mark, slowly. "It probably is just wishful thinking. It's likely they'll try to ask for something in return, and it'll almost certainly be something we're not prepared to give. Or—well, we'd be fools to ignore the possibility that it's not the Resistance at all. Maybe the EuroGov nicked it from themselves—or one of their Resistance moles has masterminded the whole thing—and it's really just an attempt by the pursuivants to snare a few Believers."

A long silence from Uncle Peter. "Heaven forbid, that never even occurred to me. Okay, now you're *definitely* not going."

"So you said already. I'm feeling better about the

decision the more I think about it, though. The perfect lure—the perfect trap. Better not to take the bait."

"Indeed. Well, talking about safety, I'd better take myself off."

"May I confess before you go?"

"Of course."

I drew away from the door quickly and ran back downstairs, Bane following, feeling a belated prick of conscience. Was eavesdropping an actual sin, or just rude? I'd have to find out.

KYLE

Bane was keen to see some action film. Margo and Father Mark were agreeable, so I nodded and smiled too, and we settled down with popcorn. It probably wasn't that terrible a film, but I couldn't concentrate on the explosions and the frantic running around.

Saint Patrick's Shamrock. Something the great Irish saint actually held and touched, centuries ago. The holiness of a saint sort of . . . rubs off . . . on such items, giving them great spiritual power—or at least making them channels of such. We had the relics in the disguised altar upstairs, of course — our house being a secret Mass center — but they were relics of recent, local saints, martyred since the beginning of the religious suppression. Such relics were, alas, all too common nowadays and therefore considered best to use in altars that in most cases would eventually be found and destroyed by the authorities.

But a really old relic. A relic of a really big saint . . . I'd never seen one, let alone touched one. How could Uncle Peter just let it go?

Not that I disagreed with him, exactly. Of course Father Mark's life—and above all, ministry—were far more important. But . . .

But couldn't *someone* go? Someone less important? What was the harm in trying? The Resistance would either turn up with the stone or they wouldn't, right?

What about someone expendable? Someone like . . . me?

A shiver ran down my spine at the thought. But I had everything I needed, right? The time, the place. Why couldn't I go?

What if something went wrong? But . . . Saint Patrick's Shamrock . . . I was so conflicted about my vocation. I felt like God was probably calling me to the priesthood, but I was so *scared*. Priests suffered the worst, most agonizing martyrdom of all. The mere thought made me sick with terror. Maybe a really, really holy relic was just what I needed. Maybe praying with it would give me clarity. Give me a spiritual infusion. A holy backbone.

Longing surged inside me at the thought. All I had to do was go get it. If I was too chicken even to do that . . . then I definitely wasn't cut out to be a priest, was I?

MARGO

Kyle didn't seem very into the movie. Eventually he excused himself quietly and went upstairs. Probably going to say a rosary or something. He prayed a lot these days, though he didn't flaunt it.

I wasn't enjoying the movie all that much. Not a lot of plot. I should probably join Kyle for his rosary. But I didn't want to hurt Bane's feelings. He didn't come for sleepovers so often, now that we were older. Let's face it, it's not so fun when you're sleeping in separate rooms and can't chat until stupid o'clock before falling asleep.

So I stuck out the film. Then we played a crazy game of snap with Father Mark until after midnight, at which point, perhaps remembering that he'd been left as the responsible adult, he called time and we headed to bed.

I couldn't settle off, though. The Shamrock of Saint Patrick! If only someone could've gone to get it. Well . . . remembering Father Mark's final analysis . . . maybe not. Still. If only we could have got it *somehow*.

Before we had the run-in with that train in the spring and I got shot in the arm, I could've imagined Bane suggesting we go get it ourselves. He'd have thought it a great adventure, even if he wasn't that interested in the relic itself. But he had actually been a bit more cautious since then—at least where I was concerned.

I was drifting in a vague fantasy in which Bane and I triumphantly presented Uncle Peter with the shamrock and he told us we'd done more for the Underground than any other fourteen-year-olds in recent memory...when a noise from outside jerked me fully awake. *Rats!* I'd almost been asleep.

Just so long as it *wasn't* rats. As in, pursuivants . . . A cold prickle running down my back, I slipped out of bed and peeped out the window. Nothing suspicious. I was jumping at shadows. Except...where was my bicycle? There was Bane's, where he'd chained it up. But not mine. The only other person who used my bicycle was . . .

Choking on a sudden lump of terror, I dashed to Kyle's room, tapped on the door and flung it open.

Empty bed.

"Father Mark!" I pounded on the guestroom door, then yelled down the stairs to the living room, where Bane had the couch. "Bane! Get up, quick! Kyle's gone to get the shamrock!"

Forty-five minutes later, the three of us were creeping along a ledge below the overlook above Caella crag, each clutching a handful of the fireworks that Bane had acquired a few months ago intending to fire them at targets in our garden—a plan that had swiftly got them confiscated and stuffed in a cupboard by my engineer-dad. Father Mark thought they might be useful for a diversion, if we didn't manage to stop Kyle. And—I glanced at my watch, five to two—that didn't look too likely now.

"Okay," breathed Father Mark, looking down into the clearing below. "This is good. If we manage to spot him approaching, we let off some fireworks in his general direction and scare him off. Otherwise . . . well, we'll be able to hear what they're saying from here, so we'll just have to see how events unfold."

Ugh, why couldn't we have got here sooner? We'd found my bicycle pulled off where we always left our bikes when we came to this area of the forest, but Kyle wasn't with it. He'd too big a start on us.

KYLE

Ahead was the clearing at the base of the crags. I checked my watch. Almost dead on two AM. I swallowed hard. Father Mark didn't think that the Resistance could be trusted. But he was sure they had the stone.

If I can do this, maybe I am fit to be a priest.

Well, if I couldn't, I definitely wasn't, anyway.

Nervously, I tugged at my balaclava with a gloved hand, checking that it covered my sweaty face, keeping my identity secret.

Okay, Lord. Here goes.

I walked forward, shielding the bulb of my torch with my fingers so only a slit of light escaped as I headed for the big boulder in the middle of the clearing. I'd barely gone two strides from the trees when I sensed movement behind me. Two men had emerged from the forest, both wearing headlights. One held a pistol, another a rifle. Where had they come from?

I turned again. What the . . .? Men—and one woman?— now circled the perimeter of the clearing. One man stood just on the other side of the boulder, waiting. Some wore balaclavas or bandannas over their faces, but he didn't. He must be too compromised to live a normal life anymore. Killers, all of them. Like dealing with the devil. Well, I wasn't here to *deal*, was I?

I marched up to the boulder. "I'm here for the

shamrock." I tried to keep my voice steady, though it chose that moment to crack annoyingly.

The man stared at me. "And who are you, little boy? I understood the message was passed to a priest."

"Why would they send a priest when they can send me?"

A nasty smile played around the man's lips. "Expendable, are you?"

"Yes," I said defiantly, though my insides turned to jelly under his cruel gaze.

"And you call us ruthless."

"Look, do you have the stone?"

"Oh, we have it." He reached out and set something tiny on the boulder. I shone the torch, my breath catching as the light bounced off smooth, green marble. I stepped forward, reaching, but the man quickly placed a hand over it. "Wait up, dove-boy. Say we talk terms."

My insides knotted up. "Nothing was said about terms. It doesn't belong to the EuroGov, and it doesn't belong to you. It belongs to us. So do the right thing and hand it over, like you promised."

"Promised is a strong word," smirked the man, taking his hand from the stone and waving it invitingly. "So let's talk terms. You look strong and sharp enough. We won't ask much. Just come on a Young Resistance op with us. Peaceful stuff, Young Resistance outings, no killing. Give your word you'll come, and you can take the stone now."

"No." I fought to keep my voice steady, eyeing the Shamrock. Would they shoot me if I just tried to walk off with it? Maybe. "I'll leave with the stone or without the stone, but I'm not going on any Young Resistance op."

The man's jaw jutted out, his expression turning ugly. But before he could speak, another guy dashed into the clearing.

"Soldiers! Great long line, trying to encircle the clearing. Closing in fast."

The leader spat a swear word. His eyes jumped to me. "Right, grab dove-boy in case we need to trade him to them."

What? Dismayed, I took a step backwards, but hands gripped me from behind.

MARGO

"I don't think so!" muttered Bane, lighting a firework. Father Mark had just lit one too and, finally getting the lighter to work, I did the same.

With a fiery hiss, Father Mark's rocket streaked downwards, followed by Bane's. Father Mark's smashed, bright and loud, into the trees overhead, but Bane's went so close to the leader he leapt back with a yell as the flaming tail scorched his hand.

As my firework detonated, Kyle twisted free of the man holding him. Two steps forward and his hand closed around something on top of the boulder. The leader reached for him, shouting—then threw himself backwards to avoid another firework from Bane. Kyle darted back towards the trail, but five Resistance guys blocked his path. He turned and bolted the other way, but yet another man went for him. I'd already lit my next rocket, but I grabbed it and turned it that way, only just snatching my hands back before it went off. Our heavy leather gardening gloves only provided limited protection.

The firework streaked low enough that the guy ducked and Kyle dodged around him, his football skills coming in handy, and pounded away into the undergrowth. But . . .

"The bikes are the other direction!" I hissed. "What's he going to do?"

"Run, I hope," said Father Mark. "And that's what we're going to do as well. Go. *Quietly!*"

Most of the Resistance were legging it, but two with rifles peered up at the crag in an alarming way.

"What about Kyle?" I demanded, as we made it off the ledge and back into the trees and started sprinting, using only Bane's red torch for light.

"This is a big forest, Margo. You and Bane know that," panted Father Mark. "There's no way we can find him. We'd just get caught ourselves. I'm sorry, but he's on his own now. He's fast and fit and has a head start; he's got a good chance."

Reaching the bikes, I started to climb on the back of Bane's while Father Mark got onto Dad's.

"No," said Father Mark, "take your own bike, Margo. Kyle's never going to get here before the soldiers do, and there'll be old fingerprints."

I wanted to argue, but . . . fingerprints. He was right. I jumped on the bike and away we went, peddling hard. Cutting across country, away from the pursuit, we eventually reached the town as the night began to lighten from black to gray.

"What do we do, Father Mark?" I asked, waves of cold shakiness gripping my insides as the full horror of the situation sank in. The soldiers would assume Kyle was Resistance—and if the Resistance got clean away, there'd be no one to tell them otherwise. Better they assume him Resistance than Underground, anyway—better for the rest of us, too. But they'd still pursue him. And if they *caught* him . . . "We can't go home, can we?"

"Not yet." Father Mark spoke calmly. "You go home with Bane to his place. I'll find a position from which to watch your house. As soon as Kyle makes it back, I'll let you know. And if it's raided, I'll call and let you know that, and your parents, too. And we can all make ourselves scarce. But try and stay calm. Forewarned is forearmed, in this sort of situation. We're not in great danger, okay?"

He was understating it a bit, and we all knew it. Not in danger of instant capture, perhaps, but trying to make it to the Vatican Free State, hunted, was not a safe occupation, and if our cover was blown as Believers, it would be our only option.

Well, Bane would probably make a Divine Denial happily enough, agnostic that he was, and, for now, I might only be sent to a juvenile detention center—but Kyle? At sixteen, refusing to make the denial and having been involved in a crime—as they would see it if they caught him with that stone—Kyle was more likely to be ruled unReformable and dismantled.

KYLE

I wasn't stumbling through blackness anymore, but grayness. The trees began to stand out black against that gray. I should've been able to make better time at the cost of fewer cuts and scrapes, but I was so exhausted by now I staggered as I ran. I'd been running for hours, surely. Dawn was coming.

Yet again, I stopped and listened. Were they still following?

The pre-dawn silence of the Fellest should've been absolute. But from way back came the sound of engines and other noise. How much of a lead did I have?

Not enough. And what if they set up a cordon ahead of me? *God, please, please don't let me be taken. I'll have killed them all, Mum, Dad, Father Mark . . . Please, please, please . . .*

What if I got rid of the stone?

I pulled it from my pocket, turning it in my hands as I stumbled onwards. *Saint Patrick, pray for me, please?* I pictured myself throwing the precious, irreplaceable object into the undergrowth and winced. But it had been lost before throughout history and always found again in the end . . . and if they caught me without it, I was just a teenage boy, right? Yeah, a boy wandering the Fellest in the wee hours of the morning. Of *this* morning. They probably assumed I was Resistance, but they'd still take me before a judge to make the Divine Denial. Ditching the stone would make little difference unless I could somehow get back to Salperton without being captured. I might as well hang onto it for now.

A noise from closer behind me brought me to a stop, my head up, listening intently. Animal? Or soldier? Another noise . . . how far away was that coming from? It was so hard to tell at this silent time of day. Too close for comfort . . .

I started running in earnest again, dodging around trees and forcing my way through bushes, the stone clutched in my hand. No, I must put it away! What if I dropped it somewhere?

As I groped for my pocket, my face caught on a branch and the balaclava was torn off. I grabbed for it with my free hand—got it—then turned, sprinting onwards . . . but my foot caught in a tree root and my momentum flung me forward down the slope like a stone from a catapult. I felt my hands open, grasping at air as my arms flung out, trying to break my fall. I saw the glint of the shamrock as it flew away from me—and I saw the pale boulder in the grass below, a moment before my head—

Crunch.
Crunch.
Crunch.

The rhythmic noise grew closer and closer, slowly penetrating both my awareness—and the pain in my head. Where was I? What was happening? I opened my eyes, then closed them as warm golden light dazzled me. Daylight. And thick grass towering above me.

Daylight? How long had I been unconscious? And what was that noise?

I dragged my eyes open again, just as a sharp metal blade parted the grass and bit into the earth inches from my nose, making me shoot upright with a yelp—or try to. I collapsed back onto my elbow, clutching my head. The spade swung high, turned from tool to potential weapon as the wielder leapt backwards.

I held up my hand in a helpless attempt to shield myself, an involuntary groan escaping my throat at the sudden movement. But it did me some good, because the spade was lowered.

"Are you all right, boy?" The man looked down at me for a moment. He sounded quite upper-class. "Well, evidently not. Can you sit up?"

Every detail of my predicament flooding back into my mind, I levered myself into a proper sitting position, looking around wildly. The edge of a forest glade. A 4X4 jeep sat on the other side of the clearing. An older man sat in the driver's seat with a large newspaper draped over the steering wheel and a thermos of coffee in one hand, though just now he was looking my way with the body language of someone considering putting aside his comforts and getting out to help.

But . . . coldness rushed through my veins. Was he wearing a . . . uniform?

My eyes flew to the man standing over me, and I squinted against the light that framed him.

Uniform. Oh God, help me! But . . . not army uniform? No.

Seeing me squinting, he stepped several paces to the

side, allowing me to see him clearly. Sleek black boots, crisp grey jacket and trousers, fancy epaulettes . . . bile rose in my throat as the identification clicked. EuroBloc Genetics Department Security. He was an officer from the nearby Facility where they sent "imperfect" eighteen-year-olds when they failed their Sorting—along with Believers—to be dismantled for spare parts. And where priests were executed the same way—without anesthetic. I was looking at the closest human thing to a monster.

But . . . was he out looking for *me*? With a *spade*? If not, maybe I could talk my way out of this.

The tailgate of the jeep was down and covered in . . . flowerpots? Well, that explained the spade, but weird.

The monster crouched, peering at my forehead with concerned eyes. "Have you been lying out here all night? You must be . . ." Breaking off as his eyes fixed on something lying on a patch of moss, he reached out and picked up a small object.

Saint Patrick's Shamrock.

My stomach knotted up as my fumbling attempts to piece together an implied account of a hike gone wrong flew to pieces. Would he recognize it?

He reached out and snagged my balaclava from a nearby twig. His eyes moved back to the stone, then to me. Oh yes. He recognized it.

Act innocent, Kyle . . .

"What's that?" I asked.

The man raised one eyebrow, as fair as his neatly trimmed hair. "What indeed? It appears to be marble, shaped—quite nicely too—like a plant. Some species of clover, by the look of it." He met my gaze again, and his eyes were hard. I'd not appreciated his concern before; now I wanted it back. "I'd say . . . a shamrock."

The man in the jeep opened his door, obviously concerned that I remained sitting on the ground, but the EGD officer waved a negating hand. The door closed again and a sip of coffee was taken, a page of the newspaper turned. But the man kept stealing looks our way. Was he a bodyguard or just a driver?

"Where did you get this?"

"Me?" I tried to look confused. "*You* just picked it up off the forest floor . . . "

He grabbed the collar of my shirt and dragged me to my feet. Despite his lean build he was tall, and surprisingly strong. When I staggered giddily, he shoved me back so that I leaned against a tree for support, panting and bracing my head against the trunk as pain throbbed through it.

Slowly, the pounding of the blood in my brain eased enough for me to hear again.

"Where did you get this?" the officer repeated.

"It's not mine." No lie. It belonged to every Believer, right?

"No, it's not, is it? Where did you get it?"

"I told you, it's not mine."

"Fine. Enough dancing around the houses. Why don't you make the Divine Denial?"

I fought to control my face, to hide my dread. What

reason could I have to refuse, *other* than being a Believer? Well, I could try for contrary, authority-hating teenager.

"Divine Denial?" I laughed in his face. "Who do you think you are, a judge?"

His lips curved up in a cool smirk. His hand went to the holster at his right hip. Came up holding a pistol. Which he pointed straight in my face. "You were saying?" he spoke silkily, but his gaze was hard. "Now, you will make the Divine Denial, or I will fertilize the forest with your brains."

Weird to see eyes such a similar shade of green to Margo's looking at me so coldly . . .

I shook free of the inconsequential thought, fighting panic. Shoot me? Unlikely, but he would take me to a judge. And if I refused to say it to the *judge* . . . then I would probably die. But not only me. Mum. Dad. Father Mark. Margo in a few years, when she was old enough to be executed. And any Believer close enough to us to be dragged before a judge as well . . .

Oh, how could this be happening?

Don't be an idiot, Kyle. This happens every day. You know that. And you know what you have to do.

But Mum . . . Margo . . . everyone else I loved . . .

A click as the man cocked the pistol. "Make it."

Maybe he really was going to shoot me. Such bleak eyes . . . Sweat trickled down my forehead into my eyelashes and a strange buzzing filled my ears. Was I going to die, right here and now? Four words, and I didn't have to die. No one had to die.

Only my soul. What choice did I have?

Breathing shakily, I raised my head and met those green eyes. "No."

Oddly, the eyes warmed. With a click as it was uncocked, the pistol went back into the holster. "So." He eyed me, head slightly to one side. "You're one of those fishy folk, not one of the bloodthirsty brigade."

My mouth dry, I couldn't speak. What did he mean? Belatedly, it came to me. Resistance or Underground. That's what he'd been testing. And apparently . . . Underground didn't bother him? Maybe he was lulling me into a false sense of security. He'd probably been involved in the deaths of hundreds, maybe thousands, of Believers. Or at least helped keep the Facility running so the executions could take place.

He opened his mouth to speak, then paused, head tilted. Listening. I listened too.

Oh no! Breaking branches. Scuffing. Low voices . . . It sounded like a whole line of soldiers. I shot a panicked glance at the officer and lurched a few paces across the clearing. *Oh God, help me!* The pain in my head spiked with each step and my balance had totally deserted me. I stumbled to a halt rather than fall down in a heap, looking wildly from the driver—watching me over his newspaper, still—to the officer, to the sounds of the searchers.

Absolutely no way I could outpace them in my condition, even if the officer just let me shamble away. I was done for.

This must be how a sick, hunted animal felt. *Lord, help!*

Putting one slender hand on his hip, the officer looked me up and down and sighed. Pocketing the stone, he jerked his head at the jeep. "Get in the back. Under the tarpaulin."

I gaped at him. Was he serious? Maybe he just didn't want to bother chasing me.

"Or not." He shrugged and turned to drive the spade into the soil again, busy excavating a short trench.

What choice did I have? The way I staggered as I started towards the jeep answered that question. No choice at all.

"Be careful of the fuchsias," added the officer curtly.

The what? Oh. Clumsily, I pushed some of the plant pots aside and dragged myself up into the vehicle, barely choking back a moan as pain pulsed through my head at the exertion. Tarpaulin—yes, there at the back. I eased myself underneath, leaving the tiniest crack through which to peer out. Would he just stroll up and fasten the tailgate, completing my capture without even having to get his underling out of the cab?

Uh-oh, twigs snapping, the soldiers were coming . . .

He was approaching, too. But he just tossed the balaclava into the back—I pulled it quickly out of sight— and re-arranged the flowerpots, so that by the time the first soldier pushed through a bush and into my field of vision, they covered the whole tailgate again.

The soldier paused, his eyes doing a double-take at the vehicle, the men, and the evidence of gardening. Finally, clearly satisfied that the uniform was genuine—the Facility wasn't all that far away, after all—he trod forward.

"Excuse me, uh, sir, have you seen a teenage boy?"

The officer turned and directed a long, scathing look at the soldier. "You do see my uniform?"

"Yes, uh, sir?" The soldier looked like he was biting into tar, using the respectful term, but was clearly too junior to dare not to. What rank *was* the officer? An army guy might know.

"Well then, do I *look* like someone teenage boys strike up conversations with?"

"Um, no. Sorry, sir." The soldier turned away and motioned his unseen companions. More smashing, tramping, snapping sounds as they ploughed their way onwards.

Well, that was a skillful bit of equivocation, no mistake! But I couldn't dwell on it. I felt . . . I felt . . . Desperately, I clawed my way to the edge of the tailgate, sending flowerpots flying, just managing to get my head out before I vomited.

Tutting softly, the officer picked up the scattered pots and returned them to the back of the vehicle, pushing them right inside.

"Very well, get yourself back under that tarp," he said, when the heaving tailed off. Then he raised his voice to address the driver. "We're going into Salperton. I need something from the garden center."

"Yes, sir."

My head hammering, weak as a rag, I crawled under the tarpaulin again. I'd no choice but to trust this . . .

monster . . . a little more. Why was he helping me? The Facility where he worked butchered kids only two years older than me every day.

Slam. Clink. The tailgate went up, and his footsteps went around to the front. The vehicle tilted and creaked as he got in. The driver's voice came through the wall to me. "What about the boy, sir?"

The officer's voice went super-bland. "Boy? What boy, Watkins?"

A moment's silence. "Of course. There is no boy. Must've nodded off for a moment and had a funny dream."

"Maybe you'd better finish your coffee before we go."

A voice was speaking. To me? Something poked me in the side.

"Come on, lad, wake up. Time to get out."

I dragged my eyes open. We were stationary. The tailgate was down again. The officer stood there. An empty road. No soldiers. Was he really going to turn me loose? *Oh, please, Lord!*

"I'm assuming you don't wish to go to the hospital?"

Hospital? Absolutely not.

"No," I croaked, crawling to the edge. "Thank you . . ." Strange words to speak to someone like him, but I had to say them.

He gripped my arm as I climbed down, steadying me. "*Can* you make it home?"

"Of course." I spoke automatically, desperate to get

away.

"All right, then. One more thing." I raised my head and peered at him through aching eyes. Oh. In his hand lay the stone. The Shamrock of Saint Patrick. Eagerly, I reached out for it, but he closed his fingers. "Fishy boy. Answer me this. Is this stone worth your life?"

My mouth opened, an indignant "yes" about to fly from my lips—but I stopped, closed it again. My *faith* was worth my life, yes. In fact—though I'd barely registered it in the turmoil of the moment—I'd refused to make the Divine Denial. I'd just faced the greatest test a Believer could face—and held firm. Incredibly.

But the stone. However holy, however precious, however irreplaceable, whatever mystic powers might be associated with it, it remained a created thing. Well, so were we all, but it was only an *object*. Was it worth more than my life? No. Was it worth more than Margo's, Mum's, Dad's, Father Mark's lives? Definitely not.

I moistened my cracked lips. Met his solemn gaze. "No."

"No. I didn't think so." He slipped the stone back into his pocket. "Go on, then. If you're stopped this close to town, it won't matter. Unless . . ." He patted his pocket meaningfully.

I took a step down the road, sick at heart but angry with myself for the feeling. I was alive, wasn't I? And everyone I loved, too. Somehow, I'd got away with it. So, I'd not managed to get the stone. It's not like Uncle Peter tasked me with retrieving it. I knew he'd have forbidden me, in fact. Maybe I'd never been meant to have it. I'd just got greedy and fancied myself a hero.

The jeep door slammed behind me, and the engine started. I concentrated on taking one step after another. How far was home from here? Dear Lord, help me, it seemed such a long way.

The jeep roared past, splitting my head open with its noise. Mist gathered, obscuring everything. Then the road began to wave up and down. Was it an earthquake? Was it . . .

My foot turned sideways and I was falling. My forehead struck the tarmac with an agonizing jolt. The mist turned into black tendrils, swirling over my vision.

The sounds of a gear-change, a vehicle reversing, echoed in my ears. A tire appeared in my vision, followed by a pair of smart, booted feet.

Then the blackness ate it all.

MARGO

The phone rang, making me start violently. Since the house still hadn't been raided, twenty-four hours later, and we were desperate for news of Kyle, Bane and I had crept back inside several hours ago, leaving Father Mark still keeping guard outside. There'd been no messages, but now I bolted down the hall and snatched up the handset. "Hello?"

"Mrs. Verrall?" An official-sounding voice. "I'm calling from the hospital. It's about your son, Kyle."

KYLE

I stared at the picture on the detective's accessor. Why did it seem so familiar?

"It's stone, right? A clover or something?" The photo was zoomed in tight on the object, but in the bottom right-hand corner was something that looked like the end of a small label. "Hang on, is this in Salperton museum?" A memory popped into my mind—a newspaper's front page, the photo, the headline . . . "Wait; this is the thing someone stole, right? A few days ago? It was in the local paper. Haven't you got it back yet?"

"No, Kyle. We haven't. Can you tell me exactly when you last saw it?"

I stared at the picture some more. *So* familiar. But I'd no memory of it. If I admitted anything . . . how might I be incriminating myself?

"Uh . . . I was at the museum . . . last year. School trip."

"You haven't seen it since?"

I stared at the photo again, fighting unsuccessfully against a yawn. My body wanted to sleep again already, despite the anxiety-inducing presence of the detective. "I don't remember seeing it, no."

"Okay. Well, thank you, Kyle. I won't keep you awake any longer."

He switched off the accessor and slipped it inside his jacket, then pulled out an omniPhone and consulted it. My eyes dragged, heavy as lead . . .

I floated around a misty forest, insubstantial as a ghost. "Dove-boy?" people were shouting, their voices harsh and cruel.

"Dove-boy, where are you?"

"Where do you want me to go next?" A voice, speaking nearby, jerked me awake again, but sleepiness held my eyes closed. "The boy's story matches that of the witness'. As one might expect, considering his security clearance. This was a waste of time."

Curiosity winning, I raised my lids just a fraction. The detective stood in the doorway, the omniPhone to his ear. I let my eyes sink closed again.

"I know, but no. You can't always tell if someone *is* Resistance, but you can tell when they're definitely not. This boy just chose the wrong day to cycle into a tree. Sounds like all they broke up was a Young Resistance meeting, anyway, and their stray got clean away. Close this case, then? What next? Uh-huh. Okay. Yes, sir. I'll be right there."

And with that, he turned and walked away.

"So? Did you get it?" demanded Bane, once I was home a few days later and it was finally safe to talk.

"Get what?"

"The shamrock!" said Margo. "I saw you grab it before you ran! Don't you have it? What happened to it?"

"Shamrock?" The detective came to mind at once and with it, belatedly, the name of the stone. "The Shamrock of Saint Patrick?"

"Yes, of course!"

"I'm sorry, Margo, I don't remember what happened at all. I was cycling along, apparently, and came off . . ."

"Cycling?" said Bane.

"No, you weren't!" said Margo. "You left my bike at Caella Crag, and I brought it home."

"No, on my bike, I presume."

"Your bike?" Margo's eyes widened. "Kyle, you sold your bike a month ago. Remember?"

Of *course*. That's what had been niggling at me for days. I didn't *have* a bike anymore. I'd sold it to put the money towards the car that I hoped might enable me to follow my vocation. If I was brave enough to go through with it.

Odd. The thought didn't seem quite so frightening as it usually did.

"I remember now. But I don't remember anything about the other night. I'm sorry."

They tried to help me get my memory back, of course. They told me every detail they remembered. They asked me a hundred questions in a hundred different ways, trying to tease the memories from my head. It was no use. Apparently, I'd had the shamrock and somehow ended up in hospital without it. And that's all we knew.

But as the leaves started to fall from the trees, I began to remember. Little bits and pieces. A tire and some well-polished boots. Running. Fear. Pain. My head striking tarmac. Striking a boulder. Small plants in little pots. Lots of them.

There was a shadowy, enigmatic figure who'd helped me, though for some reason that was extraordinary—if only I could remember why.

And I'd refused to make the Divine Denial. I remembered looking down the round barrel of a pistol and saying, "No." Warm, dizzy disbelief, relief, thankfulness, filled me every time I thought about that. Maybe I really was strong enough to be a priest. With the Lord's help.

I said nothing to Margo or Bane. The thought of them hearing how I'd refused to make the Divine Denial, the thought of their pride and admiration and awe—my insides squirmed with embarrassment. No, they thought I didn't remember. And I didn't, not properly. I was happy to leave it like that.

As the months crept on and the flow of memory snippets dried up completely, I accepted that I would never remember any more.

So, where was the precious shamrock, now? Lost to us, that was for certain. Maybe God wanted the Underground to have *me* more than he wanted us to have the relic. Like Uncle Peter said—people really were the Underground's greatest treasure.

Because the decision I'd wrestled with so long came easily, now. I told Mum and Dad I thought I might have a vocation to the priesthood. I broke it to Margo. I worked hard on my plan for faking my death. My mind was made up.

After Mass on Saint Patrick's Day, the seventeenth of March, I knelt in Adoration in front of the hidden sanctuary, my heart open before my Lord and God. And, after all the lingering fear and anxiety concerning my decision, peace finally filled me to the brim. I wasn't asleep, but . . .

Two hands, coming from crisp grey sleeves. A patch of ground. A trowel, digging a hole. And into the hole the hands placed the Shamrock. A handful of little black seeds went in on top, and the hole was filled in again.

I came back to myself with a start.

What? Was that real, Lord? Is that what my shadow-man did with it? He buried it?

Excitement flowed through me. Was the Lord showing me where it was? Could I go and dig it up?

Where, Lord? Where is it?

Eagerly, I closed my eyes and tried to calm myself, tried to make myself as still and open as I could, trying to listen.

Shoots grew up from the earth, taller and stronger. Green leaves budded forth. Beautiful hanging flowers bloomed . . .

But I could see nothing of the surroundings at all.

No, Lord. Where?

No use. No matter how hard I tried, I just saw that bush, that beautiful sentinel, growing larger and larger as the seasons cycled past—and nothing more.

Swallowing painful disappointment—*dreaming of glory again, greedy Kyle?*—I tried to think through what it might mean.

Did You want me to know it was safe, Lord? Is that all? That the man returned it to Your keeping in the most respectful way he could? And some day, when You will it, someone will find it again? But not me. You have another path for me?

Or was he just hiding it? I mean, what sort of man plants a *stone*?

Not a mere stone. The Shamrock of Saint Patrick.

Yes . . . after all, if the Holy Spirit were to water something made of stone . . .

. . . who knew what might grow?

###

Kyle, Margo, and Bane live in a future where faith is outlawed and priests and believers are hunted ruthlessly. To find out what happens when Kyle flees the EuroBloc to follow his vocation don't miss the novella *Brothers*. Or to take on the system with Margo and Bane, pick up the novel *I Am Margaret*.

ABOUT THE AUTHOR

CORINNA TURNER is the author of the I Am Margaret and unSPARKed series for young adults, as well as stand-alone works such as *Elfling* and *Mandy Lamb and the Full Moon* (for teens) and *Someday* (for older teens and adults). She has just released *The Boy Who Knew (Carlo Acutis)* the first book in her new Friends in High Places series about friendship with the saints. All of her novels have received the Catholic Writers Guild Seal of Approval (except new releases for which the seal may be in process). *Liberation* (I Am Margaret Book 3) was nominated for the Carnegie Medal Award 2016 and *Elfling* won first prize for "Teen and Young Adult Fiction" in the Catholic Press Association 2019 Book Awards. Several of her other books have been placed in the CPA Awards and the Catholic Arts and Letters Award.

Corinna Turner is a Lay Dominican with an MA in English from Oxford University, and lives in the UK. She has been writing since she was fourteen and likes strong protagonists with plenty of integrity. She used to have a Giant African Land Snail called Peter with a 6½" long shell—which is legal in the UK!—but now makes do with a cactus and a campervan. You can find out more at www.IAmMargaret.com.

BOOKS FOR TEENS & YOUNG ADULTS BY THESE AUTHORS

CAROLYN ASTFALK
Rightfully Ours

T.M. GAOUETTE
The Destiny Of Sunshine Ranch
Freeing Tanner Rose
Saving Faith
Guarding Aaron
For Eden's Sake
Shadow Stalker

ANTONY B. KOLENC
Shadow in the Dark
The Haunted Cathedral

AMANDA LAUER
A World Such as Heaven Intended
A Life Such as Heaven Intended
A Love Such as Heaven Intended

THERESA LINDEN
Roland West, Loner
Life-Changing Love
Battle For His Soul
Standing Strong
Roland West, Outcast
Fire Starters
Chasing Liberty
Testing Liberty
Fight For Liberty
Anyone but Him

SUSAN PEEK
A Soldier Surrenders:
The Conversion of St. Camillus de Lellis
Crusader King:
A Novel of Baldwin IV and the Crusades
Saint Magnus, the Last Viking
The King's Prey:
Saint Dymphna of Ireland

CORINNA TURNER
I Am Margaret
The Three Most Wanted
Liberation
Bane's Eyes
Margo's Diary
Brothers
The Siege of Reginald Hill
Someday
Drive! *(Unsparked 1.0)*
A Truly Raptor-ous Welcome *(Unsparked 2)*
BREACH! *(Unsparked Prequel)*
Elfling
Mandy Lamb and the Full Moon

LESLEA WAHL
The Perfect Blindside
eXtreme Blindside
An Unexpected Role
Unlikely Witnesses
Where You Lead

For more authors and titles, visit CatholicTeenBooks.com.
And subscribe to our newsletter for new titles *hot off the press!*